ISA & THE GUY NEXT DOOR

(THE SUNNYVALE MYSTERIES, #1)

JESSICA SORENSEN

CHAPTER ONE

I'VE ALWAYS ROCKED THE WEIRDO GENE, AND I'VE MOSTLY been okay with that. But life would be a tiny bit easier if my parents and sister marched to the beat of their own drum, too. Unfortunately, their style is more *Leave it to Beaver* with an edge.

My mom is the epitome of a Stepford housewife on crack. She can bake a cake, clean the house, put together a fundraiser for our school, and make sure my sister and I are doing our homework, all while looking perfect.

To most, my dad is the perfect husband and father. He works in the city and is the vice president of a company. He makes a decent salary, like most people who work in the city, holds a high status in the community, and gives my mother everything she asks for.

Then there's my older sister, Hannah. Growing up,

Hannah was our parents' star prodigy. From preschool up until first grade, she starred in beauty pageants and won so many tiaras and trophies my parents made a special room for them, which basically means she has two bedrooms. As she got older, she got into modeling and was even in her own commercial for some robotic gadget that was supposed to tease hair to its "fullest potential." My parents were always bragging about her at work functions and community get-togethers.

High school is where Hannah really blossomed, according to everyone. She developed an obsession with makeup and fashion, and her confidence and beauty helped her rise to the top social status tier. She became student body president, head cheerleader, and Queen of Sunnyvale—the title handed to one lucky senior who receives a flashy crown, free dinner at the club for a year, the privilege of riding on the float in the Sunnyvale Sunny Days parade, and a scholarship.

Then there's me, the baggy clothes wearing, manga loving, aspiring comic book artist, zombie enthusiast. Being different would be fine—there has to be a weirdo in every family—except mine isn't very accepting of people who can't understand, including their own daughter. A junior in high school, my greatest accomplishment is having my own blog that is just a way for me to get all the clusterfuck of weirdness out of my head.

I once beat the entire neighborhood, including the

guys, in a free throw competition. But when I do shit like that, it always earns the same reaction from my mother: "You're such a tomboy. When are you going to act like a girl?"

I clock in a lot of time reading, dye my hair an array of colors—today it's green stripes!—and doodle my own comics, starring kickass female characters who aren't afraid to be themselves, an attribute I try to live by.

Sometimes, it's hard, though, trying to find people who "get me" or whatever. I live in my own little shell as the outcast. Sometimes, I feel like I can barely breathe, like the walls are closing in. My worst fear is that I'll die in that damn shell, probably by asphyxiation.

"Why aren't you breathing?" my mom asks me from across the lengthy dinner table.

I hold my breath another few seconds before releasing a deafening exhale. "I was just wondering how long it'd take to die from lack of air." *And if anyone would notice if I dropped dead at the kitchen table.*

She stares at me, unimpressed, then shakes her head and looks over at my dad. "I really don't get her some-times." She cuts into her chicken, sawing into the meat so violently the knife scrapes against the plate. "No, I take that back. I don't understand her at all."

Hannah snorts a laugh as she taps her manicured nails on the buttons of her phone. "No one does. Just ask anyone at school."

"Hey, some people get me," I argue, stabbing my fork into my salad. "I swear they do."

She glances up at me with her brows arched. "Name one person. And the janitor doesn't count."

"I'm not counting the janitor," I say, chewing on a bite of salad. I've never understood why my sister seems to hate me so much. Ever since we were in grade school, she's made it her mission to torment me as much as she can. "Although, Del's pretty cool."

"Oh, my God, you're a freak," she sneers. "And I know you don't have friends, so don't pretend like they exist."

"Just because the people I hang out with aren't cool enough for you, doesn't mean they don't exist." I'm calm. Perfectly cool. A lazy river on a hot summer day. Because, if I'm not, if I lose my shit with Hannah, my ass will be sent to my room without dessert. And I love dessert almost as much as I love manga.

Hannah dramatically rolls her eyes. "You're so lame. At least own that you're a loner and spare yourself the embarrassment of pretending you're not a loser."

I bite my tongue to keep from firing off anything that'll get me in trouble and chant a lovely, sweet treat song inside my head.

Oreo cake. Cookie dough ice cream. Strawberry cheesecake.

"You know what?" Hannah sets the phone down on the table, and when she smiles at me maliciously, I know she's about to say something that's going to get me in trouble, that even my sweet treat chant won't save me from. "I take that back. Maybe the janitor can count. I mean, you eat all your lunches in the janitor's closet, right?"

"No," I say through gritted teeth. "And you know I don't, since you pretend to ignore me every day during lunch."

Her grin broadens at the sound of my clipped tone because she knows she's won, that I'm about to lose my cool.

She mouths, *"Loser."*

A slow breath eases from my lips, and then I stuff my mouth full of chicken.

Snickers. Chocolate chip cookies. Funnel cake—

"Oh, wait!" Hannah exclaims with a laugh. "I do remember you hanging out once or twice with that freak who always wears mismatched shoes. I think she's into girls ..." She taps her finger against her lip. "Wait, is she your girlfriend?"

I can't control it any longer. I swallow the chicken and drop the fork. "Leave Lana out of this. She's a nice person, unlike you." I drop my voice and utter the nickname I know she hates, "Super Bitch."

"Mom!" Hannah whines, slamming her palm onto the table and sending the salt and pepper shakers toppling over, along with my mother's wine. "Isa called me a bitch."

My father and mother stare at the mess on the crisp linen tablecloth. Then my mother glares at me.

"Isabella, you can go to your room now," she says as she scoots back from the table.

"But I didn't do anything." I try not to sound whiney because it'll only piss her off more. "Well, not anything that she didn't do."

"And you don't get any dessert," she says, ignoring my protests as she strides to the kitchen door.

"I'm really sorry," I tell her as calmly as I can, "but she did call me a loser."

When no one's looking, Hannah flips her blonde hair off her shoulder and flashes me a smirk. "You're such a liar."

My mother looks at my father in that way that says *you take care of her* then she slams her palm against the door and whisks out of the room.

"Isabella, your mother said to go to your room, so go to your room." He speaks robotically, as if he rehearsed the words. He avoids eye contact with me, staring down at his plate. "And no dessert."

He rarely looks at me, and I haven't ever figured out why. I asked him about it once, but he pretended like he didn't hear me and hurried out of the room, leaving me to draw my own conclusions. My very overactive imagination has conjured up quite a few borderline crazy ideas, ranging from him thinking I look like a hideous beast to him fearing I secretly possess the superpower to change anyone who makes eye contact with me into a human corpse.

Knowing there's no way my father's going to cave on my punishment since we've been in this same situation at least a hundred times, I stand up. "Okay."

"And apologize to your sister," he adds, still staring at his chicken like it's the most fascinating thing in the world.

Only when I turn my back to Hannah do I mutter, "Sorry." Otherwise, her smirk will drive me batshit crazy.

As I'm walking out of the room, my mother returns with a towel to clean up the mess, along with a platter of red velvet cupcakes.

"Why are you still here?" she asks me as she sets the platter down at the end of the table. "I told you to go to your room."

With a heavy sigh, I bid farewell to the cupcakes and leave the dining room, trying to convince myself they probably taste like burnt cardboard, even though my mother's won ribbons for her fan-freakin'-tastic cupcakes.

An hour later, I'm sprawled across my bed, surrounded by homework, my sketchbook, and a few of my favorite novels. My Chemical Romance is playing from the stereo, and my balcony doors are open, letting a warm May breeze blow inside.

I'm still trying to convince myself that my parents don't hate me. That all their anger and bitterness toward me is simply because they don't understand me. That their partialness to my sister has nothing to do with me. But it's hard when my dad won't even look at me, and every time my mother speaks to me, it's either to ground me or to tell me what a disappointment I am.

I lie in bed, lost in thought, until my belly grumbles. God, I wish I could at least have just a taste of those red velvet cupcakes. However, if I'm caught sneaking into the kitchen, my butt will be grounded. It might be worth it because seriously, my body's about to have a lack-of-sugar conniption fit.

Ugh!

I roll off my bed and do an awesome zombie impression as I crawl across my floor toward my dresser. "Must … get … sugar …"

When I reach the dresser, I hoist myself to my feet and raid the top drawer for some old Halloween candy I stashed there months ago. I find a half-eaten bag of jelly-beans and a half-eaten chocolate bar that doesn't have a wrapper, and I devour both of them.

Turns out the chocolate bar has the gross addition of almonds. I instantly dry heave, realizing why the candy bar was only half-eaten to begin with.

"Gross!" I search for a trashcan to spit it out. I have no clue where mine ended up, though, so I trip out onto the balcony and spit out the mouthful of candy over the edge.

It takes me about two seconds to realize what a stupid idea that was for three different reasons:

1. My sister is hanging out in the driveway, which is right below my window.

2. The chocolate I just spit out has landed on her head.

3. She's talking to our neighbor, Kyler Meyers.

Kyler Meyers. What can I say about him other than he's gorgeous, popular, the star quarterback, and smart? Like, he takes AP classes and has a 4.0 GPA kind of smart. I'm also in love with him, have been since I was eight years old and he stopped Hannah's ring of minions from picking on me during recess.

"Hey, just leave her alone," he said when he stumbled across us at the playground.

They had me trapped on the top of the slide and were threatening to push me down it. It wouldn't have been a big deal except there was a giant mud puddle at the bottom. Somehow, Hannah had managed to scare all the rest of the kids away, so no one was around to witness what was about to go down. Even the recess monitor was MIA.

Hannah had crossed her arms and raised her brows at Kyler. "Why're you sticking up for her, Kyler? She's a loser." She stepped toward him and batted her eyelashes.

"How about you just go back to playing football with your friends and leave us alone?"

Kyler glanced at me then around the empty playground. For a moment, I thought he was going to bail. Then he stepped around Hannah and her friends and offered me his hand.

"Come on, Isa."

I took his hand, and he helped me to my feet.

When they'd chased me up there, I'd fallen down and scraped up my knees, but I hardly felt the pain as he held my hand and guided me off the playground.

He only let go of my hand when we were a safe distance away from them.

"Are you okay?"

Unable to find my voice, I nodded.

"You should try to stay away from her," he said, looking over his shoulder at Hannah and her crew, who had targeted a new victim.

"Okay." I managed to get one word out and was super proud of that.

He offered me a smile before heading back to the field to play football with his friends, oblivious to how much his good deed meant to me. It was the first time someone had stuck up for me. Ever. And I've been in love with him ever since.

I know my crush won't ever go anywhere. I guess I'm a glutton for punishment. Deep down, I get that I'm not really in love with Kyler, especially since sometimes he does things that make me hate him. But in love sounds so much less porn star-ish than *in lust*.

The playground isn't the only time he's done something nice for me, though. There's so much more to my "in lust" crush than that.

When I was in eighth grade, he gave me a rose on Valentine's Day.

"Hey, Isa, I have something for you," he said as he jogged across the middle school parking lot toward me.

I paused when he said my nickname and gaped at him spastically with half a brownie in my mouth. He was a year older than I was, and I couldn't figure out why he was talking to me. Not only was I Hannah's loser younger sister, but I was also in middle school, and he was in high school.

"Happy Valentine's Day." He stuck out his hand, his fingers wrapped around the stem of a red rose.

I cautiously glanced from the rose to him then gulped the brownie down. "Is this a trick?"

Chuckling, he brushed his brown hair out of his eyes. "Why would I ever want to trick you, Isabella? I have no reason to."

My insides quivered at the sound of my name leaving his lips. The last time he had any social interaction with me was in third grade.

My gaze darted around the mostly vacant parking lot

as I searched for a blonde-haired girl hiding out some-where, laughing her ass off.

"Did my sister put you up to this?"

He swiftly shook his head. "I swear to God it's not a trick. I just wanted to do something nice."

I still didn't take the rose, worried the moment I accepted his gift, my sister would show herself and laugh at me. Knowing her, she'd probably have her Super Bitchy Cheer Pod People with her, who'd be ready to take pictures of my mortification.

"Isa." He dipped his head to make eye contact with me, not because I'm super short—I'm actually above average height—he's just, like, one-step-away-from-not-making-the-parking-garage-clearance tall. "I swear to you this is just one neighbor giving another neighbor a gift with no tricks attached."

A neighborly gift? I almost frowned, but it was a completely selfish, Hannah-like reaction, so I sucked it up, took the rose, and even managed a smile.

"Thanks."

He smiled, and my heart did an Irish tap dance. "You're welcome." He didn't leave right away. "Hey, so I have to ask you for a favor." He paused, hesitant. "And you can totally say no, but ... I really need to work on my free throw for tryouts next season, and since you won that contest and were pretty badass, I thought you and I could practice together. Maybe you could teach me a few pointers."

Is Kyler seriously asking me to help him improve his basketball skills? I wasn't sure how I felt about that. On one hand, I was excited that I had an opportunity to spend time with him. On the other hand, it made me feel like he saw me as one of the guys.

"Sure," I replied with a small smile.

"Thanks." He looked relieved. "Wanna meet at my house tomorrow morning?"

I nodded, and he threw me another smile before he turned around and headed toward the football field located between the middle school and high school.

I stared down at the rose, wondering what the gesture meant—if it meant anything—and spent the next couple of weekends obsessing about every other gesture he did during our practices. Like, when he brought me a doughnut or we spent a couple of hours after practice watching a movie. Part of me wonders if he was just being friendly, while another small part of me hoped it meant more.

He even opened up to me a time or two.

"Sometimes, I feel like I have to be good all the time, because that's how everyone expects me to be," he muttered after his dad had come home and spent over a half an hour critiquing Kyler while he made basket after basket.

"I'm sure no one expects you to be that way," I said as we sat on his porch steps, drinking lemonade, our clothes soaked with sweat. "No one can be good all the time."

"Yeah, I know." He scratched his arm, staring at the driveway. "Sometimes, it feels like the whole school doesn't see it that way. Like I have to be that guy who takes the team to the championships, who gets good grades, who's happy all the damn time, even when things get shitty. My parents expect that, too." His hand fell to his lap and he caught my gaze from out of the corner of his eye. "My dad especially. Sometimes, it feels like he's trying to live his dreams through me. Sometimes, I wish I could just stop."

"Stop being that guy?"

"Stop being the guy who's happy all the time and just be normal."

"Normal is overrated," I mumbled. "Trust me."

"Yeah, maybe. But I'll never know, since I've never felt like anything about my life is normal." He sighed tiredly then shook his head. "You probably think I'm a douchebag, sitting here complaining about my perfect life."

"You're fine. It's okay to complain about life. Everyone gets tired of being who they are at some point." I picked at my fingernails. "And it's okay to change. You know, if you really want to."

He only nodded with his brows furrowed, like the

idea greatly confused him. Then he released a breath and leaned back on his elbows. "Thanks for being such a great listener." He leaned over and did something amazing. He kissed me on the corner of my lips. "You're so much different than anyone else I know. I feel like I can be myself when I'm around you."

His words meant a lot to me, but the kiss damn near caused me to stop breathing. It was more than just magical. It was out-of-this-realm amazing. The problem was, once he got better at free throws, we stopped practicing, and our movie/doughnut/heart-to-heart time ended, too.

Kyler went back to being the perfect, popular guy everyone expected him to be. Yeah, he still smiled and waved at me whenever he saw me and talked to me during school sometimes, but that was about as far as our friendship ever went. He still sticks up for me, though, when someone is harassing me at school.

"What the hell was that?" Hannah combs her fingers through her hair. Then her face pinches in disgust as she stares at the chocolate in her hand. "Oh, my God! Is that bird shit!"

"Um." Kyler hesitantly glances up at me, and then his gaze drops to her hand. "It could be," he says, even though he witnessed me spitting it out.

He glimpses up at me again, and we exchange a look. I know he won't rat me out. He's not like that. He's still that nice guy who wins championships and gets good grades, the guy who everyone loves, and who I know secretly wishes he didn't have to be. Although, I sometimes wonder if he still wants to be different. Over the years, he's seemed to grow into his position as being the popular guy everyone loves.

"Isa!" Hannah screeches from the driveway, jerking me away from one of my favorite memories. "Are you listening to me?"

"I wasn't, but now I am," I say, blinking at her.

She grunts, stomping her foot again. "Did you just spit something in my *hair*?"

Call it payback for that stunt she pulled at the dinner table, but honestly, I don't feel that bad.

"Sorry. The candy had almonds in it, and I panicked." I shrug. "I really hate almonds."

"Oh, my God! You're such a freak!" She stomps her feet several more times, throwing one of her infamous beauty queen tantrums.

I feel sickly satisfied when Kyler covers his mouth with his hand to hide his laughter.

"I'm going to get you back for this," she threatens, crossing her arms and giving me her notorious death glare. "Just wait. When I get done with you, even the janitor's closet isn't going to be safe."

"Hey, calm down." Kyler touches her arm. "It's just candy. I'm sure it'll wash out. And Isa didn't mean to. I saw the whole thing. It was an accident."

I kind of wish I really was a zombie so I could have a legit excuse to shimmy down the railing and gnaw off her arm he's touching.

Hannah takes a few breaths with her eyes narrowed on me, and then she spins toward Kyler, plastering on a plastic smile. "Wait for me while I go wash my hair. Then we can leave for the party."

"Sure. I'll just go shoot some hoops in my driveway or something." He backs down the driveway toward the end of the fence.

Only when he turns his back to us does Hannah lock her glare back on me. *"You're dead,"* she mouths.

Eventually, she'll make due on her threat, probably at school when I least expect it. God, how I wish UW was farther than a ten-minute drive, and she had to go live at college. But nope, she's staying here, at least for a while.

Le sigh. *Story of my life.*

I probably should be majorly concerned over what she's going to do to me, but honestly, my reputation at school can't get any worse. So, I focus on something better, something that'll cheer me up.

My attention wanders to Kyler as he rounds the fence. Then my smile plummets when I notice him checking Hannah out. It's his one fault and something I don't get. Yeah, I know she's beautiful, curvy, has long, blonde hair, and dresses like a girl. Back in grade school, though, he seemed disgusted with her. Sometimes, he still does, like the time she tripped Jane Tribloton at a pep rally in front of the entire school. Kyler went and helped Jane up, and then I caught him chewing out Hannah in the hallway later on in the day. Those moments remind me of the Kyler I first fell for. Then there's this other side, the one cracked out on guy hormones.

I frown as Kyler continues to check Hannah out. God, she'd swoon herself to death if she knew he was drooling over her ass like he is. She's been trying to get him to ask her out for the last month, ever since her break up with The Brad—a nickname he gave himself.

While Kyler and Hannah aren't officially a couple, they spend a lot of time together. If they do start dating, I'll have to gouge my eyes out, so I don't have to witness them making out. Of course, if he actually starts dating my sister, I just might be able to finally get over this silly, little crush I have on him.

"Isa, are you okay?" Kyler shouts as he bounces a basketball in his driveway while looking in the direction of my balcony.

I shrug. "Yeah. Sure."

"She's always so hard on you," he says, jumping to make a shot. As he moves, his grey T-shirt rides up just enough to give me a sneak peek at those superhero abs I know he has hiding under there.

"Who, my sister?" I ask distractedly as I discreetly check him out.

Stop staring at him, for the love of God.

The ball swishes through the net, and he turns back to me, smiling adorably. "Yeah. I mean, I like her and everything, but she's nice to me. With you, she always seems so …" He seems to be searching for the right word.

"Bitchy? Vile? Or how about plotting-my-death, off-the-rocker, Norman Bates kind of crazy?" I offer, resting my arms on the railing.

"Well, I was going to say intense, but those work, too." He's trying really hard not to smile.

"Can I ask you a question?" I dare ask, despite the inner voice screaming at me to keep my trap shut.

"Sure." He offers me an easygoing grin.

"Why do you like her? I mean, she's so mean … and you're so …" I stop myself from saying nice because I'm uncertain how he'll react.

"I don't know. I just …" He glances at the door to my house then rubs the back of his neck, looking really uncomfortable. "Isa, I don't really feel comfortable talking to you about this."

Give me a crown, people, because I just took the title for Most Super Awkward Girl Ever.

Thankfully, the side door of his two-story house swings open, and out walks Kai, Kyler's younger brother, who's a junior in high school like me.

He's not wearing a shirt—he usually isn't—his boxers are sticking out of his black cargo shorts, and his light blond hair is smashed on one side, as if he just woke up. The whole sleepyhead, rebellious look he's rocking is a recent change, as well as the people he started hanging out with—the stoner kids, labeled as such for wearing dark clothing, eating a lot of junk food, and their overall don't-give-a-shit attitude. At least, that's what everyone calls them, although I have yet to see any of them smoking pot. If that were the case, then I'd be a pothead, since the description fits me, too.

"Hey, what's up?" Kai gives a chin nod to Kyler as he closes the door behind him.

"Not much," Kyler says to his brother as he picks up the basketball. "I'm thinking about heading to a party."

"Which one?" Kai asks before stuffing a spoonful of cereal into his mouth.

He shrugs, dribbling the ball against the concrete driveway. "I think one of Hannah's friends is having one."

He chokes on a laugh and spits out a mouthful of cereal. "Sounds like tons of fucking fun." Sarcasm drips from his tone.

"It won't be that bad." Kyler lifts his arms up to shoot another basket.

"It'll be a bunch of dumbass cheerleaders and jocks," Kai says, setting his bowl down on the porch railing.

"I don't know what your problem is." Kyler walks backward toward the grass to collect the ball. "You used to be one of those"—he makes air quotes—" 'dumbass jocks' too, before you decided you were too good for everyone."

"That's not what quitting the team was about," Kai replies in a clipped tone. "So stop talking about shit you know nothing about."

"Then what was it about?" Kyler challenges as he scoops up the ball and tucks it under his arm.

Kai shrugs, picking up his bowl, looking pissed off. "Who cares?"

"Whatever, man." Kyler's gaze bores into Kai, like he expects him to cave. "You know everyone thinks you're into drugs now."

Kai lifts his shoulders and shrugs again. "That's their problem. Not mine."

"I'm starting to wonder if they're right."

Kyler sounds more aggravated than I've ever heard him. And trust me, I've eavesdropped on his conversations a lot, so I would know.

They argue for a few minutes longer, acting completely like night and day. Kyler and Kai may be brothers, but they sure don't act like it. Yeah, Kai is equally as gorgeous, in a dangerous, bad boy, let-me-stun-you-with-my-smoldering-eyes kind of way. Up until about six months ago, he used to be almost as good at football as Kyler is, and nearly as popular. He even flirted and checked out Hannah sometimes. Then, one day, he did a complete one-eighty, quit the team, and started spending a lot of time ditching school. I always thought it was odd that Kai was the one who went the route Kyler once wanted—well, in terms of changing. I'm not really sure Kyler ever wanted to become a rebellious bad boy.

The one thing that remained Kai, though, is he's really intense, to the point where looking him in the eye can actually be terrifying for some. And for some girls, exhilarating. For me, not so much because, unlike a lot of people, I know there's a dorky side to Kai, one who thinks he's funny and who reads comics.

"Believe whatever you want." Kai backs toward the porch, shrugging off Kyler. "Have fun at your lame-ass party."

Kyler dribbles the bejesus out of the ball. "Whatever. Avoid the problem, like you always do." Another slam of the ball. "Cause more problems between Mom and Dad."

Kai seems oddly satisfied by the fact his brother is annoyed with him, and a smile touches his face as he spins for the door. Right before he walks inside, though, he looks over his shoulder at me.

I should probably duck for cover since I've been caught eavesdropping red-handed. If it had been Kyler, I'd be so mortified that I'd probably bolt back to my room. With Kai … well, he and I sorta have this thing going on, ever since seventh grade. Not a relationship type of thing or anything. It's more like a "he teases me and annoys the crap out of me" thing. I don't know why he's so persistent about doing it, other than maybe I'm the only person who doesn't get all squirrely every time he looks at them.

I carry his gaze for a beat or two longer, and the smile on his face grows. I narrow my eyes at him and flip him the middle finger, just because I can. He laughs then winks at me before disappearing inside his house.

I check out Kyler one last time before I return to my bed to finish my drawing of Zombie Artist Girl, who looks great in a cape and can behead a zombie like a badass mofo.

But, the second I plant my butt down on the mattress, my bedroom door opens.

I prepare myself for an argument with Hannah, figuring it's her coming to chew my ass out for the chocolate incident. Instead, my mom and dad walk in.

I give them both a puzzled look. They hardly ever step foot in my room, let alone together.

My mom scans all the movie, comic, and band posters hanging on my black and violet walls then rolls her eyes at one of my sketches, or what she calls my "coloring book drawings."

"What a waste of time," she mutters, shaking her head.

I blow out a breath, trying to let her disapproval breeze past me. But the lack of air sensation appears as my lungs tighten and the shell I live in shrinks even more.

"Did you guys need something?" I close my sketchbook to avoid anymore of her insults.

Her cold eyes land on me. "Turn the music down; we need to talk."

I look over at my dad, who's staring out the window, his eyes all lost, scared puppy wide.

Something's up.

"Okay." I tear my attention off my dad as I reach over to turn down the stereo. "What's up?"

She presses a glance at my dad, but his eyes are fastened out of the window.

"Do you want to tell her, or should I?"

When my father doesn't budge, she huffs, snapping her fingers.

"Henry, we agreed to this, so either you can tell her, or I can."

My dad rubs his hand over his head then looks at me. Or, well, the space around me. "Isabella, your mother thinks—" My mom clears her throat, and my father adds, "Your mother and I were thinking that you should live with your grandmother for the summer."

"For the *entire* summer?" I ask, shocked.

"You'll go in a couple of days when school gets out," my mom says, smoothing invisible wrinkles out of her pencil skirt. "And you can return here to finish up your senior year."

The way she words it is confusing, like they're kicking me out, yet allowing me to come back to finish school. I'm not sure how I feel about this.

"Which grandmother?"

My dad clears his throat. "Grandma Stephy."

I relax a bit. If it was Grandma Jane, my mom's mom, then it would've been an entirely different story. The woman criticizes me even more than my mom does, so much that I sometimes refer to her as *Grandma Jane, Isabella Ego Slayer.*

"Okay, I'll go." And, hey, it might be good to get a break, if for nothing else than to get away from Hannah and whatever death-to-Isabella tactics she has planned for the summer.

"Of course you'll go, since it's not a choice," my mom snaps. "We didn't come in here to ask you to go. We came in here to tell you that you're going to go, that we need a little break from your sarcasm, your rudeness, and your"—she waves her fingers at my worn-out sneakers; holey, a-size-too-big jeans; and my oversized hoodie— my typical outfit—"whatever the hell this disaster is."

"Honey, easy." My dad glances at me, throwing me off with the brief eye contact. "She's just a kid."

She points a finger at him. "Don't you *easy* me. I've had

enough of this." Her finger moves to me. "Enough of her. And quite frankly, enough of you. I need a break from one of you, so it's either you or her, and I'd really prefer her." She spins on her heels for the door. "This was never part of the deal, and I want it fixed." She storms out of the room.

"What deal?" I ask my dad, confused. What deal did my mom make that has to do with me?

My dad's gaze bounces back and forth between me and the doorway. "Sorry, Isa. I really am," he mutters before rushing away with his shoulders hunched, cowering like a dog with his tail between his legs. He stops in the doorway for a second to say, "Call your grandmother. She wants to talk to you about taking a trip overseas, if you're up for it. Don't tell you mother, though; otherwise, she might not let you go do some-thing so ... fun." Then he hurries out of the room like it's on fire.

I take a few measured breaths then flop onto my bed and hug Mr. Scribbles, a teddy bear my dad won for me at a carnival when I was about five. It was during the one and only birthday he and I spent together.

The day had been absolutely magical, full of spun sugar, bright lights, and the chiming of games. I felt like I was floating on clouds ... until we got back to the house, and my mom yelled at him for over an hour because he missed one of Hannah's beauty pageants. The only way she let him off the hook was when he promised that he would, "Never do such a selfish thing again." That was around the same time he stopped making eye contact with me.

I never figured out why he stopped looking at me, why he seems to hate me, why my mom has always loathed me. Then again, maybe there isn't a reason. Perhaps I'm just a terrible daughter.

I set the bear down and roll over onto my stomach, battling back the tears as I work on my comic book drawing. It's one of my personal favorites, mostly because it stars my alter ego, who's much more ballsy than me. I have a sidekick, too, a woman who I sometimes like to pretend is my mom. She treats me fantastically and always tells me, *"Great job!"* every time I kick ass. I actually draw the woman a lot. She's been stuck in my head for as long as I can remember.

Sometimes, she even makes appearances in my daydreams, where she takes me to movies, out shopping, and sometimes, we just spend the entire day riding the Ferris wheel. She never gets angry with me or makes me feel small and insignificant. She even tells me she loves me.

I wipe a few stray tears from my cheeks then close my sketchbook. I've trained myself pretty well not to get too emotional over the stuff they say to me, especially my mom, but I'm not a super robot immune to such human emotion. I'm a seventeen-year-old girl who knows she's not the best daughter who, yeah, tests her parents' patience a lot; and who probably spends way too much time drawing comics and watching cartoons. Still, I want to, just once, hear them say *I love you.*

My dad said it a couple of times when I was younger, but it's been a while. And I'm almost sure my mom has at some point. It's been so long I can't remember. I've started to fear maybe there's something wrong with me that makes me so unlovable.

"It's not you. It's them," I try to convince myself as I curl into a ball with the teddy bear.

As I lie by myself in my room, though, something I do almost every day, I have to wonder if I'm wrong.

Maybe there really is something wrong with me.

CHAPTER TWO

MY DAD WAS RIGHT. MY GRANDMA STEPHY DOES WANT ME to go overseas with her.

"Are you sure you don't mind if I go with you?" I ask her the next morning before I head to school.

"Why the hell would I?" she asks, being her blunt, doesn't-give-a-shit self. "Besides, if you go, then I'll have someone young and fun to hang out with other than those old biddies."

"Wait? Old biddies? Who are we going with?" I dig through my dresser, looking for a clean T-shirt. Unable to find one, I end up rummaging one out of the hamper.

"The rest of the Sunnyvale Bay Community."

"So a bunch of old people?" My mood deflates. Then I remind myself it doesn't really matter who I'll be going with. Anything is better than being home.

"Hey, I'm not old!" she argues. "Not even close."

"Sorry." I grab my sneakers from the closet. "I didn't mean you. I know you're not old."

"Good girl," she says. "Now, make sure to pack light. I don't want to be hauling around a bunch of clothes, shoes, and shit we don't need. Makes the suitcases too heavy and hurts my back."

"All right, I will. And thanks again for letting me go with you."

"I'm glad you're going, Isa. We're going to have a lot of fun."

After I say good-bye, I hang up, change my shirt, and put on my sneakers. Then I run a brush through my tangled hair, pick up my bag, and head for the door to go to school, wondering what I've gotten myself into.

Going on a trip overseas sounds like a blast, and I can handle going with Grandma Stephy. But going with an entire a group of senior citizens … I wonder if I'll be the only teenager there.

Oh, well. It doesn't really matter. I don't exactly have a choice either way, so I might as well make the best of the situation. And, hey, maybe a break from my family will be a good opportunity to do some soul searching without the worry of being scrutinized.

OVER THE NEXT FEW DAYS, I finish final exams during the day while packing my bags at night. I spend a whole five minutes saying good-bye to the few friends I have. I'm not super close with anyone, and the see-ya-laters are a depressing reminder of just how much of a loner I am.

My parents go back to barely speaking to me, although my sister's been overly chatty. She even convinced her Cheer Posse to do a cheer for me when I was walking across the gym, and then they laughed at me.

I still don't really understand why they were laughing. They were the ones who looked like morons bouncing around with pom-poms and chanting a cheer, rhyming dork with joke and spelling my name with a z.

By the time I'm actually loading up my stuff to go to my grandma's, I'm stoked to be getting away for a while, even if it's on a three-month trip with people five times my age.

"Do you have everything you need?" my dad asks as he loads the last of my suitcases into the back of our SUV.

I nod, staring at the front window of the house where my mother is watching me with her arms crossed.

"I should probably go say good-bye to her, right?"

He shuts the trunk of the car, steps back, and tracks my gaze to the window. "Maybe you should just wave good-bye. Might be easier, since she's so upset."

"Why is she even upset with me? I didn't really do anything but argue with Hannah."

"That's not what this is about." He struggles for words and to look at me. Finally, he manages both. "It's just hard for her sometimes. I think this trip might help ... ease some of the tension." He pats my arm, causing me to jump, and he jerks back. "Sorry." He massages the back of his neck, squirming. "I'm just going to go tell her we're leaving. Then we'll hit the road. We can even get some ice cream on our way out, if you want."

Normally, I'd be all over the offer to stop for sugar, but even cookie dough ice cream can't melt the fact that my own mother doesn't want to say good-bye to me.

I slump against the back of the SUV. "Okay. Sure."

He hesitates, his lips parting like he's about to say something. Then he decides against it, rushes up the driveway, and hurries inside the house.

A few seconds later, my sister pulls up in her shiny silver Mercedes. She honks her horn, scaring the living daylights out of me before she turns off the engine and climbs out.

"A little jumpy, aren't ya?" she sneers as she bumps the door shut with her hip. "I guess I'd be, too, though, if I was getting kicked out of the house."

"I'm not getting kicked out of the house. I'm just going to visit Grandma."

"Keep telling yourself that. I seriously wouldn't be

surprised if I never saw your pasty face again." She slings the handle of her purse over her shoulder and starts up the driveway. Then she pauses and shoots me a smirk. "Oh! I completely forgot to tell you the fabulous news."

She may think she's perfect, but she's not, I try to convince myself. *See the lipstick on her teeth? It looks like she fed on someone's blood. Plus, her hair looks kind of frizzy today, like she stuck her finger in a socket.*

I shake my head at myself. Who am I kidding? She's perfect, albeit evil. Still, that doesn't seem to count for much with the people I go to school with.

"Kyler and I are officially a couple." She flips her hair off her shoulder, her smirk growing.

"Huh?" I blink at her. What the hell did she just say?

"Kyler and I are a couple." She enunciates each word. "You know, our next-door neighbor, who you've been in love with since forever."

My jaw nearly smacks the concrete. "I-I'm not in love with K-Kyler."

"Oh, please. Everyone knows you've been in love with him since he gave you that stupid rose, which, FYI, was a pity gift."

I want to tell her she's wrong, that I was in love—in lust—with Kyler before that, but that would only confirm her accusation that I'm in love with her new boyfriend.

Oh, my God.

Reality slaps me hard across the face, and my stomach

twists. It's not like Kyler hasn't dated anyone before. He's had a few steady girlfriends over the last couple of years, and I've always handled that pretty well. But dating Hannah? God, I knew it might be coming, but deep down, I think I was in denial, naively believing that Kyler would never date a person who is so ugly on the inside.

"He told everyone the next day that he gave you the rose because he felt sorry for you." She covers her mouth when my expression sinks. "Oh, my God, you didn't know that? That's so sad." She lowers her hand. "And tragic. I can't believe you'd ever think he'd love someone like you." Her face twists with disgust. "That god-awful hair. Seriously, who puts green in their hair? And those clothes"—she shudders—"so gross."

"I'm not in love with Kyler," I argue, breathing in and out, trying to fight back the waterworks. "So none of what you're saying matters."

Let her words roll right off you. She's not a good person.

"You're such a bad liar. Always have been." She turns her back on me and strolls toward the door, her four-inch heels clicking against the sidewalk. "And for the record, Kyler's an amazing kisser." She giggles to herself before going inside and shutting the door.

I ball my hands into fists. "One of these days, I swear to God I'm going to …" I trail off as I feel someone watching me.

I glance over at the Meyers' house then internally

cringe. Kai's sitting on the back porch, staring at me. He's wearing a pair of black board shorts, his hair looks damp, and those intense eyes of his are practically boring a hole into my head.

Shit. Did he just hear all of mine and Hannah's conversation? Fuck it. Does it really matter? I'm sure Hannah's already pretty much told Kyler I'm obsessed with him.

"You're going to, what?" Kai asks with his head cocked.

"Huh?"

My stomach flips with nerves. If he knows I like Kyler, he's never going to let me live it down. That's what Kai has been doing for the last six months—teasing me whenever he sees a good opportunity.

His lips quirk like he's fighting back a laugh. "I was just wondering what you were going to do to your sister." He nods his head at the door. "You never finished your thought, and I'm really curious what your twisted mind is going to come up with this time."

My lip curls. I'm not sure if he's teasing me or being serious. I never do with him.

"I didn't finish my thought because I was trying to make it really good, like sickly morbid and full of torture. But thanks for ruining my train of thought."

He chuckles. "I'm going to miss this."

My brows dip. "Miss what?"

He raises his head, grinning, and for some reason, that only pisses me off more.

"Our lovely little chats."

I stare at him, unimpressed. "Is that what you call torturing the nerdy next-door neighbor?"

He presses his hand to his chest. "I've never tortured you. That's your sister's thing, not mine. I've always been nice to you."

A disdainful laugh escapes my mouth. "Like the time you told me the stripes in my hair made me look like a rainbow?"

"Hey, rainbows are cool." He seems totally amused and has his smoldering let-me-bind-you-in-place gaze going on. It's driving me absolutely crazy, and I become desperate to win our little argument.

"Okay, how about the time you ate my science fair project?"

"Hey, who puts chocolate on their science fair project?" He gapes at me. "Seriously, that was your own damn fault."

Okay, he has a point. The chocolate volcano project was kind of a disaster.

"How'd you know I'm leaving?" I change the subject, wandering toward the fence.

"You mean, besides the suitcases you just loaded up in the back of the SUV?" He cocks his brow, but underneath the surface, he abruptly grows uneasy, fiddling with the leather bands on his wrists.

"You heard it from someone." I eye him over with suspicion. "I can tell. You got all squiggly."

He rolls his eyes like I'm being ridiculous then surrenders. "Fine, your sister's been telling everyone."

"That I'm leaving?" My brows knit. "Why would she do that?"

He scratches the back of his neck, looking everywhere except at me. "Um … well … she's been telling everyone that you're being admitted to a mental institution, but I know that's not true."

Invisible pins stab my skin. I don't want to hate my sister … I really don't … but I kind of do right now.

"Why'd she say I was going?" My voice sounds so hollow.

"That doesn't matter." He rises to his feet, steps off the porch, and strides over to the fence. "Where are you going, though?"

"Overseas with my grandma, which probably sounds lame, but I'm actually looking forward to it."

"It doesn't sound lame at all."

"Not even the going-with-the-grandma part?"

He shakes his head, waving me off. "Nah, grandmas can be cool sometimes. Is yours?"

"She's, like, the queen of cool grandmas. Seriously. She's the one who taught me how to drive. And I'm talking, like, floor-your-car-to-the-max kind of driving. She taught me how to swim too, in a pool that was closed. We had to sneak in through this hole in the fence. She even let me try beer for the first time." I pause, realizing something. "You know, without her, I might have ended up lacking a lot of necessary life skills. Well, besides the drinking beer part. I don't think that's a life skill."

"Oh, that can be a life skill," he assures me with a devious grin, and I repress one of my own, not wanting to encourage him. "She does sound pretty cool, though."

I bob my head up and down in agreement, fully aware of how lucky I am to be going on this trip with the coolest grandma ever.

"You'll have to post some pictures so I can see all the awesome things you do," Kai says, squinting against the sunlight.

I snort a laugh. "Oh, Kai, you and your silly, little jokes. We both know I'm not cool enough for social media."

"That wasn't meant to be a joke." He stuffs his hand into his pocket and retrieves his phone. "But if you're really that anti-social, I'll give you my number and you can send me all of your awesome photos. It'll make me feel special, too."

I roll my eyes but give him my number so he can text me his. I don't really think he's going to do it, but two seconds later, my phone vibrates from inside the pocket of my jeans.

"Have fun on your trip. And I mean that, Isa. Have fun. You deserve it, more than anyone." He gives me a strange look as he puts his phone away, like he can't quite figure something out. Then he swiftly clears his throat. "Yeah, but the whole point of me coming over here was to give you a little advice."

I pull a wary face. "I'm not sure I want to hear your advice."

He offers me one of his infamous sexy, playful pouts. "Why not?"

"Because …" I sigh heavy-heartedly when his sexy, playful pout turns into genuine sulking. "Fine. You can give me advice, just as long as it's not an 'it'll get better after high school' speech. I don't want to hear any of those. I've heard too many."

"It's not one of those, I promise. Cross my heart and hope to die. Stick a needle through Hannah's eye." He draws an X across his chest, giving me a lopsided grin.

I can't help grinning goofily back at him.

"I'm surprised you remember that."

"Of course I remember that," he scoffs. "We used to say it all the time."

"Yeah, but that was a long time ago, back when we were actually kind of friends."

An awkward quiet fills the air between us as the past hovers over our heads.

See, once upon a time, Kai and I used to hang out. And not in the way Kyler and I hung out for a few weekends while I helped him improve his free throw skills, and he opened up to me once. Unlike Kyler, Kai and I were actually friends. Well, sort of.

For most of seventh grade, he walked home with me after school. He always seemed sad about something as we strolled up the sidewalk toward his house. While I could never figure out what had him feeling so blue, I did learn some stuff about him that no one else knew. Like, how he's secretly into comic books, likes zombie movies, and listens to '80s punk rock.

During the time we spent together, I always tried to cheer him up. It was the least I could do for him not being too embarrassed to walk home with me. Sometimes, my jokes made him smile. Other times, he seemed too stuck in his head. Even if the walk was filled with quietness, it was still nice to have a friend.

After a few months of walking home together, he started hanging out with me on weekends. We'd mostly stay in my room, and sometimes, we'd go to the park. I was really starting to believe we had a chance at becoming real, seen-in-public friends. Then came the dreaded day when one of his friends caught us hanging out at the park, and he started making fun of Kai for "being in love with a loser." Kai panicked and told his friend I was stalking him, and that was the last time we walked home together.

"My advice was actually about your sister," Kai says, breaking the silence between us. "I was going to say you need to do something to get her to leave you alone. You've put up with her shit for too long."

I stuff my hands into the pocket of my hoodie. "When you say *do something to get her to leave you alone*, are you talking like mafia-style, or like, how Penny Milerford got Nora Benninting to leave her alone by punching her in the face? Because I'm not a mobster, nor a crazed honor roll student who may or may not be on crack."

"Penny isn't on crack. That's just a stupid rumor." His expression hardens as he backs away from the fence. "People need to stop spreading shit around about other people just because they think something's wrong."

He starts up the porch stairs, shoving his phone into his pocket and knocking something out in the process. The object hits the ground, and I realize it's a flash drive. Why he's carrying around a flash drive in his pocket is beyond me. I don't think too much of it, though, until panic flares in his eyes as he hastily scoops it up and rushes up the back porch of his house.

Weird, but whatever.

"Oh, yeah ... and, Isa?" he says from over his shoulder. "I meant for *you* to do whatever *you* feel you need to do to get Hannah to stop treating you so shitty. Stand up for yourself, okay? She's not any better than you, no matter what she thinks."

"Since when are you so anti-Hannah? You used to flirt with her all the time."

That's the thing with both Kyler and Kai. While Kyler is mostly nice to me, and Kai spends a lot of time teasing me, neither of them have shown me the attention they've shown Hannah. Over the years, particularly when we all got in high school, both of them spent a ton of time flirting with her and her friends, checking her out, and trying to get her attention.

"I only flirt with her when I'm bored," Kai says, seeming bored right now. "But I get that she's a bitch. And I haven't liked her since I …" He trails off, though I know what he was going to say. *Since I went off the deep end and went all bad boy.* "But, anyway, have fun on your trip." He winks at me, going from serious to joking in two seconds flat. "And bring back something super cool for your most awesome, super sexy next-door neighbor."

"Huh? Who am I supposed to bring the present back for?" I glance around, pretending confusion.

His eyes narrow to slits, yet he grins. "You know exactly who I'm talking about. The guy who fills up all of your dreams."

"You mean Johny Pakerson?" I feign innocence.

He snickers. "I forgot about your little seventh grade

crush on that douche." He pauses. "You're still not into him, are you?"

"I'm more into him than my cocky neighbor next-door," I quip with a sassy smirk.

His eyes darken as he backs away from me. "You know, if you bring me back a present, it means that's not true. That you do really like me." He winks at me again then walks into the house before I can get another word out.

His advice echoes in my head.

He may joke around a lot with me, but when he gets all serious, he actually gives pretty good advice.

I make a vow to myself right then and there that, when I get back from this trip, things will change. I'm not sure how it's going to happen, but if I can survive seventeen years of being picked on, I sure as hell can figure out a way to finally make it stop.

CHAPTER THREE

I'M STILL TRYING TO CREATE AN AWESOME PLAN ON HOW TO get Hannah to respect me when my dad returns to the car.

"Ready?" he asks as he fishes the keys from his slacks.

Nodding, I hop into the passenger seat.

My thoughts remain stuck in Awesome Plan Land for most of the thirty-minute drive across town. The only time the quietness is broken is when we stop at the drive-thru to get ice cream like my dad promised, and he asks me what flavor I want.

By the time we pull up to the Sunnyvale Bay Community, I'm still lost on how to make Hannah see me differently. It doesn't seem possible, considering I'm basically trying to figure out a way to get Hannah, the Wicked Wench of the Anders' House, to be nicer to me.

No, I can do this, I tell myself. *I need to be more optimistic. I have a whole three months to figure this all out.*

The Sunnyvale Bay Community looks like an ordinary apartment complex, except all the tenants are fifty-five and over. Grandma Stephy moved here about a year ago after my grandpa passed away from cancer.

While my grandpa was a man of few words, he was probably my favorite family member besides Grandma Stephy. Whenever I visited, he'd take me down to the gas station to buy a soda and candy. We'd cruise on the back roads in his old truck, listening to old country singers, mostly Hank Williams and Johnny Cash, with the windows down, even if it was wintertime.

He never took Hannah with us; said she threw too many tantrums.

Our drives always made me feel special, like someone actually wanted to spend time with me, like I was more than just Hannah's dorky little sister who no one ever wanted around.

Man, I really miss those days and our drives.

"I'll get your bags if you want to go up," my dad says, interrupting my thoughts as he parks the car.

"Sure. Sounds good. Thanks." I climb out of the car then head up the path to my grandma's apartment.

I knock before opening the door and strolling inside. As I step over the threshold, my shoe bumps into Beastie, my grandma's fat, old calico cat, and I fall flat on my face.

The cat hisses at me, like the crabby old fart he is.

"Dammit, Beastie," I curse as I roll over onto my back, rubbing the knee I banged against the floor.

He growls and the hairs rise on his back as he scurries at me with his claws out.

I scramble to get to my feet, but right as his claw is about to reach my leg, a pair of hands wrap around his belly.

"Now, Beastie, I thought we talked about this." My cousin Indigo, who's two years older than me, scoops up the cat and lifts him, so he's eye-level with her. Looking him dead in the eyes, she lectures, "It's rude to trip people then try to eat their faces. You're not a zombie. You're a cat."

Beastie hisses at her in response.

Sighing, she sets him back down on the floor and offers me her hand. "I've been telling Grandma Stephy that she needs to teach him some manners. She says it's useless, that he's too old and already stuck in his ways."

"She's probably right."

When I take her hand, she helps me to my feet. I massage my achy knee.

"Don't take this the wrong way, but what're you doing here? I thought you were in New York attending art school."

"I was." She tucks a strand of her blood red hair

behind her ear and fiddles with one of her gauges. "Some stuff came up, though, and I had to leave."

"Did you move back home?"

"Nah, my parents didn't want to"—she makes air quotes—" 'encourage my dropout behavior.' I think they thought, if they didn't let me move back in, I'd go back to school." She rolls her eyes as she drops her hands to her sides. "I tried to explain to them that I didn't dropout, that the school decided it was probably for the better if I take a permanent sabbatical. But you know parents; they hear what they want to hear." She glares at Beastie as he hisses at her from underneath the coffee table. "Thankfully, Grandma Stephy took me in until I can figure out what the hell I should do with my life."

I want to ask her what she did to get kicked out of school, but I don't know Indigo that well. Her mother is my father's sister, and the two of them rarely speak to one another other than when we're at family reunions, and even then, the conversation is strictly formal. And my mom refuses to speak to most of my dad's relatives, saying they act like a bunch of hippies.

All I really know about Indigo is that she's into art and self-expressionism through painting and her body. I once heard her call her body a canvas. She has tons of tattoos and several piercings, and she does all sorts of crazy stuff with her hair, even shaving her head one time.

"So, are you looking after Grandma Stephy's house

while we're gone?" I ask, stealing a butterscotch from the candy dish.

She shakes her head, flopping down on the floral sofa. "Nah, I'm going with you guys." She kicks her boots up on the coffee table and crosses her legs. "I figure a little trip overseas might lead me down a path to self-discovery."

"Don't let her fool ya with her artsy-fartsy talk," Grandma Stephy says as she enters the living room. She's cut her hair since the last time I saw her but is still rocking the grey. She's never really dressed very grand-mother-ish and is decked out in a pair of rhinestone jeans and a pink T-shirt. "The reason she's going is to see Peter."

"Who's Peter?" I peel the wrapper off the candy and pop the treat into my mouth.

"Some guy she met in New York who, I guess, lives in London," Grandma Stephy explains as she opens her arms to give me a hug. "Enough about Indigo. I've heard enough about British guys to last me a lifetime. What I really want to hear about is you." She wraps her arms around me and gives me the first hug I've had in months. "How you holdin' up, honey?"

"I'm okay." I hug her back, getting a whiff of hairspray and floral perfume. It makes me smile because it's so her and it reminds me that I'm here, with her, for the next three months, where maybe I won't feel like such an outcast.

"It's going to be okay," she tells me, patting my back.

"Um, thanks." I pull back, sensing something's off. "Is something wrong? You seem a little ... I don't know, sad."

She eyes me over. "I was just going to ask you the same question."

Okay ... what the hell is going on?

"Isabella's fine," my dad insists as he walks in and drops my suitcases on the floor. He locks eyes with Grandma Stephy and gives her a pressing look. "You and I need to talk privately about what to say and what not to say. I know how much you like to run your mouth."

My grandma shakes her head at my dad. "Good grief. Sometimes, it's hard to believe I raised you."

My dad looks taken aback. "What the hell's that supposed to mean?"

She narrows her eyes at him. "It means you've turned into an asshole over the years you've spent with—"

"Don't you dare bring my wife into this," he warns, his face reddening.

"I wouldn't have to if she didn't ..." She trails off, glancing at me with worry.

The two of them arguing is nothing new, yet the way they keep looking at me, like I've suddenly started glowing neon green and sprouted an eye in the middle of my forehead, is definitely out of the norm.

"Fine. You want to talk privately, then come on." Her voice is cold, her expression hard as she turns and storms down the hallway.

My dad marches after her, fuming mad.

Moments later, a door slams shut, though I can still hear their muffled voices.

"What do you think that was about?" I ask, turning to Indigo.

She shrugs with her brows furrowed. "I have no idea." Her eyes light up as she plants her feet on the floor. "But I know how we can find out. Come on."

I reluctantly follow her as she hurries down the hallway toward where my dad and grandma went. As we near the bedroom door, their voices grow louder and clearer.

"Are they yelling at each other?" I whisper to Indigo as we stop in front of the door.

She nods as she presses her ear to the door. "They've been doing it a lot lately on the phone, too," she whispers. "I'm not sure what it's about, though."

"Can you hear anything?" I whisper, inching closer.

She puts her finger to her lips, shushing me. "I think …" She doesn't finish her thought, driving me mad. Mad, I tell you!

I press my ear to the door and listen for myself.

"You have no right to do this," my dad growls, sounding more furious than I've ever heard him, including the time he yelled at me for sneaking a sip of his scotch. "She's not your child."

"Well, she's barely yours with how shitty you treat her," Grandma Stephy barks back. "You hardly know that girl at all."

"That's bullshit. I know her better than you. She's my daughter, not yours."

"Okay, Mr. Know-it-all. If you know your daughter so well, tell me what her favorite manga book is. Or, hell, just tell me her favorite book." Silence stretches between them, and she adds, "You don't know shit about your daughter. But I do. I know she draws her own comics. And while I don't always understand them, I know a talented artist when I see one. Did you know she writes her own blog? She's pretty clever, too. Plus, on top of that, she's a straight-A student ... but I'm sure you know all this already, right?" Sarcasm drips from her voice like thick globs of honey. "I mean ... she is *your* daughter."

The silence that follows makes my stomach churn as reality crashes down on me. I always knew my father wasn't that interested in me, but the fact that he has no damn clue what makes me tick hurts like a blow to the jugular.

"You know it's hard for me when it comes to her," my father says, speaking more calmly. "And there are circumstances that—"

"I don't give a shit about the circumstances," Grandma

snaps. "When you chose to keep her with you, you chose to be her father. If you couldn't handle what that entailed, then you should've let her come live with me like I offered. But no, you decided to take her in and treat her like shit."

I jerk back from the door. "What the hell?" I say louder than I mean to.

Indigo captures my arm and tows me back down the hallway, making a beeline for the front door. I don't know if my grandma or dad heard me, but the bedroom door is still shut by the time Indigo drags me outside. She only releases me when we've crossed the parking lot and reached the tree area across from the apartment.

"Holy shit." I run my fingers through my hair as I pace back and forth across the grass. "I don't get what just happened. I don't ... None of this makes sense." I place my hands on my hips and hunch forward as my stomach burns. "*Keep me?* He chose to keep me ...? I don't under-stand." I peer up at Indigo, who has a cigarette between her lips and a lighter in her hand. "Do you know what any of that was about?"

She cups her hands around the cigarette then lights it. "I'm not positive, but I have a few theories," she says, a cloud of smoke circling her face. "But they're just theo-ries based on shit I've heard my mother and father talk about."

Still woozy, I squat down and inhale deeply. "What are the theories?"

"I'm not sure I should tell you," she says, eyeing me warily. "You already look like you're about to hack your guts up."

"I feel like I'm going to hack my guts up."

"Here." She crouches down in front of me and offers me her cigarette.

I scrunch my nose. "I don't smoke."

"I know, but a drag or two might help you chill out."

The smoke burns my nostrils as I take the cigarette from her hands. My fingers shake as I lift the end to my lips and inhale.

"Holy shit, that burns," I say through a fitful of coughs as my lungs drown in smoke.

Indigo laughs in amusement as she removes the cigarette from my hands. "Sorry. I probably should've warned you first. I thought going in blind might make it more exciting for you." She sits down in the grass and takes a few drags as I catch my breath.

Once I no longer feel like a ninja used my lungs as a punching bag, I settle in the grass beside her.

"I wanna hear your theories. In fact, I *need* to hear them. Otherwise, I'll come up with my own, and my head is full of all sorts of crazy already."

She sighs heavily. "I was hoping the whole smoking thing would distract you from that."

Shaking my head, I pick at the grass. "How can I think of anything else when it sounds like I was … adopted?"

"Is that what you think that was about?" she asks, squinting at the highway in front of us.

"Um, yeah." I massage my temples as my head pulsates.

All this time, I knew I didn't quite fit in with my family, that I was an outcast, different. And yeah, the thought crossed my mind that maybe I was adopted, but the thought was never out of seriousness.

"What else could it be?"

She grazes her thumb across the end of the cigarette, scattering ashes all over the grass. "It could be adoption … or it could be that maybe your …" She looks at me with pity in her eyes. "Have you ever wondered why your mom treats you like shit?"

"You've noticed that?"

"Isa, everyone who's ever crossed paths with the two of you knows there's tension between you and your mother."

"Tension from *her*," I point out. "I try to be nice, but she acts like I'm some sort of vile reptile or something."

She puts her cigarette between her lips, and smoke laces the air as she gazes off at the highway again. "I have this theory that maybe the reason she's always treated you like shit is because maybe you remind her of a shitty time in her life … Maybe something shitty your dad did to her that kind of led to the procreation of you."

It takes a second or two to process what she's implying.

"Wait … You think …" I shake my head. "No, there's no way. My dad didn't have an affair … He wouldn't do that to my mom, trust me. He does everything she says. Sometimes, too much."

Her brows arch. "He wouldn't, huh? Okay, I guess my theory's wrong."

I shake my head, while inside, the wheels are turning. All those times my mother looked at me with such disdain, and sometimes jealousy, are starting to make sense.

"I know this isn't what you want to hear," she says then mutters, "Although, I don't know why since your mom's a bitch." She clears her throat. "You have to admit it kind of makes sense."

I lower my head into my hands. "None of this makes sense. Where did you even get this theory? Did you just pull it out of your ass, or is it based on some sort of legit info?"

"I heard a rumor," she says. "Or, well, I overheard my mom and dad gossiping about your family once, and my mom said something about the 'other woman,' and how it was a good thing your dad didn't leave you with her."

Wide-eyed, I lift my head and gape at her. "How long ago was this?"

She shrugs as she puts the cigarette out in a patch of dirt. "I don't know. Like, a few years ago or something."

"Why didn't you ever say anything to me?"

"Isa, this is, like, the longest the two of us have talked. Usually, at reunions, your family stays in a hotel and spends a whole lot of time sitting around in the corner with your noses stuck in the air like a bunch of snobs."

"My mom makes me do that." It hits me as I say it, like a bull charging straight into my stomach. "Wait. Am I even supposed to call her *Mom*?" I push to my feet and pace in front of Indigo, reaching full-on crazy panic mode. "Or am I supposed to call her Lynn. Oh, my God, I just realized that my sister's middle name is after my mom's first name, yet I'm named after no one. It has to be true." I crouch down again as my legs turn into Jell-O. "I don't even know who my mom is."

"Hey, chill out." She scoots toward me to catch my gaze. "My theory is just a theory. And I should probably tell you that I had a theory that Grandpa was reincarnated into Beastie." She smiles as I blink at her.

Wow. She sounds as crazy as ... well, me.

"What? They have the same eyes, okay? And you have to admit it'd be pretty cool if reincarnation existed."

"That mean, old cat isn't Grandpa," I say. "But I get

what you're saying. I need to get some answers before I have a meltdown."

"Or, you could just skip the meltdown and use this as an opportunity," she suggests with a smile.

"An opportunity for what?"

"To take a self-discovering journey."

"I already know who I am."

She inspects my outfit with her brows raised. "I'm not sure I agree with you."

I tug on the bottom of my hoodie. "Just because I dress a little different doesn't mean I don't know who I am."

Her head slants to the side as she studies me. "Okay, answer this for me: what's the most exciting thing you've ever done?"

"I don't know." I try to think of something, and it's pretty dang sad how hard it is to come up with anything. "I entered a comic book contest once. That was really cool."

"I'm not talking about doing stuff that's cool. I'm talking about stuff that's exciting. Like, screaming-at-the-top-of-your-lungs-at-a-concert exciting. Dancing-in-a-room-full-of-people-like-no-one's-watching exciting. Or sporadically taking a trip to nowhere with no plans other than to drive." She smiles as she gets a faraway look in her eyes. "Or, like being kissed in the rain by a total stranger you have no plans of calling again." She looks at me, grinning. "That one I plan on doing while we're on this little trip."

"How do you know it's exciting if you haven't done it yet?" I ask, tucking my feet under me.

"Oh, Isa, the fact that you ask that means you haven't nearly experienced enough in your life. Life is all about the experiences, the good ones and the bad ones." She stands to her feet, yanking me with her. "Stick with me, and I promise that'll change."

I *almost* open my mouth to tell her I don't want to change, but then I remember her theory, and my grandma and dad's argument rings loudly in my head.

What if Indigo is right? What if my entire life has been a lie? What if the reason my mother—Lynn—has always liked Hannah more is because Hannah's her daughter and I'm not?

"Okay, I can try to do more things that are exciting, but what about the theory?" I ask as we cross the parking lot.

"What about it?"

"How do we find out if it's true?"

She links arms with me. "We're going to do a little research. And if all else fails, we'll wait until Grandma Stephy gets good and drunk, and then get her to spill the beans." She grins deviously. "You know she's a talker when she gets too tipsy. Plus, people tend to get a little crazy when they're on vacation, especially out of the country."

"Grandma Stephy is already a little crazy," I say with a small laugh, but it hurts to smile. Hurts to think.

She chuckles. "Yeah, so just think how crazy she's going to get while we're chilling in London or Paris. After a few glasses of wine and a little pushing on our part, we should be able to get the truth out of her." She pats my arm. "We'll get to the bottom of this, I promise. And we're going to teach you what excitement is."

I nod, silently vowing to go along with the plan. Inside, however, I'm terrified. What if it's true? What if I don't even know who my own mother is?

CHAPTER FOUR

A WEEK LATER, I'M CHILLING OUT ON THE BALCONY OF A very nice hotel room, staring out at the sparkling lights of the Eiffel Tower. I'm half-listening to Indigo plot out our plan to weasel the truth out of Grandma Stephy, who's downstairs at the bar having drinks.

Ever since I discovered I might not know who my real mom is, my head's been stuck between reality and daydream land, where my mind creates all kinds of scenarios on where this is all going to go, where I'm going to end up if I find out I've been living a lie. I keep replaying all the times my parents acted strangely around me, including when my dad didn't even hug me good-bye before he left Grandma Stephy's.

"Have fun, okay?" he said as he walked toward the front door to leave. "And take care of yourself."

I forced a stiff smile. "Okay."

He gave me an awkward pat on the arm before rushing out of the apartment without even saying good-bye to Grandma or Indigo.

"It's going to be okay," my grandma said with a tense smile. Then she clapped her hands together and made herself smile for real. "All right, you two. Let's finish packing. We leave really early Monday morning."

And that was that.

The last seven days have been filled with packing, driving to the airport with a bus full of older people, taking the twelve-hour flight to Paris, and getting to the hotel. We've been here for over a day, spending a lot of time catching up on sleep. After sleeping for most of the day, I now feel super awake and night has just fallen.

"I was thinking tonight might be the best night to put our plan in motion." Indigo balances an ashtray on her belly then kicks her feet up on the railing and takes a drag of her cigarette. "I know we just got here and everything, but I don't think we should waste any time. You're already stressing out way too much as it is."

"I'm not stressed … I've just been thinking." I try to focus on her and the conversation. "And which plan are we talking about? The excitement one, or getting Grandma drunk?" I fan my hand in front of my face to cool off.

In Sunnyvale, June temperatures usually hover in the

seventies, maybe the eighties, on a super intense day, and the nights bottom to forty. Right now, it's eight o'clock and feels like it's ninety degrees outside.

"We aren't going to get her drunk. We're going to wait until she gets herself drunk. And we might not have to wait that long." She taps her cigarette against the ashtray before placing it on the table next to her. "Dude, did you see all the mini bottles she drank on the plane?"

I giggle. "Yeah, I know. I can't believe she was playing a drinking game with her friends."

"I think it's so cool. I hope I'm that cool when I'm old." She lowers her feet to the ground, leans forward in the chair, and rests her arms on the balcony railing, staring over the edge at the sidewalk below. "I was talking about your self-discovering journey." She pauses, musing over something while puffing on her cigarette. "I think we should start tonight, but not go too crazy." She seems to be talking more to herself than to me. "We have to ease you into this."

"I know I'm not the most exciting person ever," I say, "but I've done some exciting things. You don't have to go easy on me."

She gives me a sidelong glance. "Careful, Isa. Giving me free reign like that can end up being dangerous."

I roll my eyes. "It's just partying. What's the big deal?"

"I'm not just talking about partying; I'm talking about completely letting go. Of everything." She stares me down, like she's trying to get me to take back what I said. I don't crack. Won't. I've spent way too much of my life doing that, something I've painfully become aware of over the last week. A slow smile curls her lips. "All right, let's do this, then." She jumps to her feet, wanders back into the room, and begins rummaging around in her suitcase.

"What are you doing?" I ask as I walk into the room.

"Making you club-worthy," she says as she sorts through her dresses, shirts, and shorts.

I grow nervous as she holds up a tight red dress that looks like it will barely cover my ass.

"No fucking way." I shake my head. "I can't wear that."

She frowns. "Why not?"

"Well, for starters …" I rack my brain for a reason other than saying I'll feel like an idiot. "I haven't shaved my legs."

She flicks her wrist, motioning me to get a move on. "Well, hurry up and do it, then."

I nervously pick at my fingernails. "I, um, didn't bring a razor."

She looks at me with confusion then suddenly relaxes. "Oh, I get it. You've never done any of this before, have you?"

I cross my arms, feeling absurdly self-conscious. "Done what, exactly?"

"Shave. Put on makeup." She shoves the red dress at me. "Dress up."

"I've never really cared about my looks, and I've never really been into girlie stuff." I pause, feeling idiotic. "And it's kind of hard, you know, to ask my mom—Lynn—to show me how to put on makeup and all that fun stuff when I know she'll probably just laugh at me and tell me how ridiculous I am to think that'll help my looks."

Like she did the one and only time I asked her to buy me a dress. I was twelve, and it was for the seventh grade dance. I thought I'd dress up, since I heard most of the girls were.

Lynn laughed at me when I asked.

"Don't be ridiculous. You'd look hideous in a dress," she said.

I fought back tears. "I think I should try to dress up. I mean, everyone else in my grade is."

She turned to me with a dead serious expression on her face. "Isabella, I'm going to tell you something that you're not going to like hearing." She hesitated, almost as if she were backing out. "You're too gangling and homely to be dressing up. You should just stick to the baggy jeans and hoodies. It suits your body type better."

As I recollect the memory, I wonder if that was the starting point of my baggy jeans and hoodie obsession. Sure, I wore them before, but not because I felt like I had to. I just didn't know how to put together an outfit. Plus, they were comfortable to wear while I was playing basketball.

After Lynn told me that, I felt as if I had to dress in baggy clothes, like I wasn't good enough to dress nicely.

What if that's the real reason I do a lot of things? What if my general weirdo-ness was created around things my mom—Lynn—said to me? Like, when she told me no one wanted to be friends with me because I was too strange. What if I stopped trying to make friends because I believed no one would want to get to know the weirdo, freak I was led to believe I was?

Pity briefly flashes in Indigo's eyes. Then the look swiftly vanishes as determination fills her expression. She strides across the room, opens the mini-fridge, and grabs a bottle of wine. Using an opener, she removes the cork then takes a swig straight out of the bottle.

God, if Lynn were here, she'd have a fit with the lack of class Indigo is showing right now.

Indigo hands it to me, and when I hesitate, she says, "No one's around. We don't need to be classy."

"That's not why I'm hesitating." Sighing, I grab the bottle, take a drink, and then give the wine back to her.

She sets the bottle aside then grabs my arm and pulls me toward the bathroom door.

"What are we doing?" I ask as I hurry after her.

"I'm giving you a little lesson. Take notes, because I'm

only going to do this once. You can't figure out who you are if I'm doing it for you."

TWO HOURS LATER, I'm walking down an overly packed sidewalk with smooth legs and tweezed eyebrows, wearing a red dress I can barely breathe in.

"Come on, Isa," Indigo says, motioning me to move quicker as she walks ahead of me. "If you keep walking this slow, the clubs are gonna be closed by the time we get there."

"I'm trying." I shuffle after her, trying not to roll my ankles. "These heels suck though."

She slows to a stop at a street corner and sighs as she leans down to untie her boot. "Come on, take them off. I'll trade shoes with you."

I stop beside her and grab the street post to get my balance. "I thought you said heels weren't your thing." Which really confused me, since she packed six pairs.

"I said most of the time they aren't my thing." She slips her foot out of the boot then unties the other one. "It doesn't mean I never wear them."

We exchange shoes, and I feel ten times better in the clunky boots. "I think I'm a boots kind of girl, for sure."

"I agree." After Indigo slips the heels on, she does a little spin in her dress. "How do I look?"

"Amazing," I say as I finish tying the boots. "I like how the flowers on the shoes match your hair."

"Me, too." She studies me with her head cocked to the side. "God, you look so great. It's amazing what a little eyeliner and lip gloss can do. Well, that, and my ever-so-awesome talent."

I stand up, self-consciously tugging at the hem of the dress. "I honestly feel kinda silly. Like I'm trying to play dress up or something." My gaze sweeps over the crowd of people walking around us. "I feel like everyone thinks I'm an impostor."

She shakes her head with a smile on her face. "Trust me, Isa; no one thinks you're an imposter." She grabs my hand and pulls me with her as she moves with the crowd again.

We walk for what feels like hours, taking in all the closed stores, the bars, the Arc de Triomphe, and the twinkling lights of the Eiffel Tower.

"Let's go up there," she says as we gawk up at the tower that stretches toward the night sky.

"I thought we were going to a club?" I ask as I rush to keep up with her.

"We can go to a club anytime!" she shouts over the music playing from a street band. "Going up there"—she tips her head up toward the sky—"now *that's* a once-in-a-lifetime excitement."

When we reach the ridiculously long line, I head

toward the end, but Indigo has other ideas and starts searching the line for cute guys who will let us cut in front of them. It takes her three tries to find a couple of guys who even speak English. They let us get in line in front of them then Indigo spends the next half-hour flirting with one of them while I stand there awkwardly.

"You look nervous," one of the guys whispers in my ear, causing me to jump. "Are you afraid of heights?"

"Um, yeah, sure." I pretend that's the reason I have goose bumps sprouting across my skin, when really it's the guys, the social interaction, the dress—everything, really.

He slings an arm around my shoulders. "Don't worry; I'll protect you." He flashes me a dimpled grin. "I'm Jay, by the way, but you can call me your protector."

I resist an eye roll. *Seriously, dude, those lines can't possibly work.* Then I pause, realizing, *Holy shit, this guy is hitting on me.*

While I'm flattered, I have absolutely no interest in Protector Jay By The Way, who kind of smells like cheese. I can't help thinking of Kyler and how he smells so good all the time; never like rancid cheese. I wish he was the one with his arm around me, but no, he's probably back home, making out with my sister.

My mood nosedives and smacks against the ground like a squashed bug. *Yuck. Why the hell did I have to think that?*

Between the mental image and Jay By the Way's cheesy smell, I feel like I'm going to hurl. I want to slide out from under Jay's arm and get some fresh air, but I can't think of an excuse that won't make me look completely deranged, so he ends up keeping his arm there until we go through security.

While Jay's emptying out his pockets, I bolt for the stairs.

"Hey, Isa, wait up," Indigo says as she chases after me.

I pause at the bottom of the stairway and wait for her to catch up. When she reaches me, out of breath, I give her an *are you kidding me* look.

"What's that look for?" she asks innocently as she fans her face with her hand.

"Those guys were gross and smelled like bad cheese. Seriously, if that's your definition of excitement, then count me out."

"That's not even close to what I meant by excitement." She kicks off her shoes and tips her head up to take in all the stairs.

"We could take the elevator," I say, eyeballing her bare feet.

"No way. That's like cheating the excitement." She steps back with her heels in her hands then sprints forward, laughing as she charges up the first flight of stairs. "Race you to the top!"

Laughing, I barrel after her and up the stairway.

People skitter out of our way as we jog side-by-side up each flight of stairs. With each step, I feel closer to soaring, closer to flying away from reality, like I'm outrunning my problems.

By the time we arrive on the second floor, though, we slow down to a sluggish walk, because, holy crap, there are a lot of stairs.

"My feet hurt," Indigo gripes, catching her breath. "But this makes it totally worth it."

"Holy shit, this is so cool." I slip my fingers through the railing and stare down at the glittering city stretched out below us."

"It's more than cool. It's exciting." Indigo reaches into her purse and fishes out her phone as I shut my eyes and breathe in the cool air kissing my cheeks.

While it might seem lame to most, tonight has been one of the best nights of my life. I've never run around and had fun without worrying about being judged by my sister or scolded by my mom.

"I feel so … I don't know … free," I say as I open my eyes.

"That's how you should feel all of your life." She leans in close to me and snaps a picture of us with her camera phone. "Look how good you look," she says as she admires the picture. "And happy."

As I examine the photo, I think about all the family photos on the wall back home, most of which don't include me. The few my mom let me be in, I never smiled, mostly because I felt uncomfortable, like I didn't belong.

"I do look happy, don't I?" I smile at the girl in the photo, a girl who only hours ago didn't exist. "Thanks, Indigo, for everything."

"Dude, we're only getting started." She puts the phone away, and then we turn back toward the view. "By the time this trip is over, there are going to be so many pictures of you smiling you're going to be posting them for days."

I don't bother telling her that I don't have a social media account, that I don't have friends, so there's no point. Maybe when I get home, I'll change that, too. Maybe I'll change everything. And maybe that change will finally make Hannah see me differently.

The plan is far from perfect, but standing up on the Eiffel Tower, stories high from the ground, anything feels possible. I wish I could hold on to the moment forever, but then we have to leave, and with each step down the stairway, I feel the perfection fading as I head back down to reality.

The feeling only magnifies when I reach the bottom, and my phone vibrates from inside my jacket pocket. Digging it out, I check the message and my stomach drops.

Unknown: Have you figured out the secret yet?

CHAPTER FIVE

By THE TIME WE MAKE IT BACK TO THE HOTEL ROOM, MY grandma is waiting for us, and she doesn't look very happy. Me, I'm not feeling that fantastic, either. And not just because of the wine I drank. The text weighs heavily in my mind as I question over and over again who sent it and why. And what did they mean by *have I figured out the secret yet?* Are they referring to the secret about my real mom, or was the text simply a wrong number? It did come up as unknown, and I don't know anyone with an unknown number.

The more I think about it, the more I don't think the message could be coincidental. The text had to have been sent by someone I know and someone who knows about my mom.

"Where the hell have you two been?" Grandma Stephy

asks the second we walk into the hotel room. She stands up from the bed, swaying to the side, a little tipsy. "It's late."

"Um …" I glance at Indigo for help. "We were just out walking."

Indigo slips her purse off and sets it on the table. "Chill, Grandma Stephy. We just went and did a little sightseeing."

She scowls at us. "You should have told me you were leaving. I was worried sick."

"We honestly thought you wouldn't even notice." Indigo flops down on the bed and yawns. "You've been super busy with your friends."

"Of course I noticed. I'm old, not blind." She inches toward me, and I can smell the alcohol rolling off her. "I promised your dad I wouldn't let you wander off."

"Really?" A smile starts to touch my lips. *My dad cares about me?*

But then Grandma Stephy hesitates, and I know she's lying.

"He really didn't say that, did he?" Sighing, I sink down in a chair to untie my boots.

"He might not have said it, but he *would* kill me if anything happened to you."

I keep my head down, focusing on unlacing the boots. "What were you and my dad talking about while you guys were in your bedroom?"

Indigo lets out a cough. "Not right now. She's too upset."

"What do you mean, *not right now. I'm too upset?*" Grandma Stephy asks, sounding drunkenly confused. When neither of us responds, she warns, "Okay, one of you two better start talking. Otherwise, I'll ground your asses to the room for the rest of the trip."

"I'm nineteen," Indigo says, pushing up on her elbows. "You can't ground me."

"And I'm sixty and don't give a shit how old you are," Grandma Stephy snaps. "I'll ground you if I want to."

Indigo tenses and keeps her trap shut.

I want to back off, too, but now that I've opened Pandora's Box, there's no going back. All these words just keep pouring out of me.

"Is my mom …? Did my dad …? Who's my real mom, Grandma Stephy?"

Her eyes widen, and I literally feel the perfection and freedom I felt on the Eiffel Tower go *poof.*

"I heard some of the stuff you and my dad said, and … Lynn isn't my real mom, is she?" I ask, sounding eerily calm. "That's why she hates me so much."

Grandma Stephy's lips part before she rapidly shakes her head. "No, I'm not going to lie to you anymore. I told your father I was sick of this bullshit and that it was time to tell you, that they couldn't just keep treating you like crap, that it is time. And I meant it."

She sits down in a chair beside me and squares her shoulders. "Isa, I love you to death. You need to understand that, okay? I love you so much, and you're my fantastic, wonderfully weird, keep-me-on-my-toes granddaughter. Your grandpa loved you, too. He even told me once that you were his favorite."

"Hey," Indigo says then holds up her hands. "You know what. Never mind. I'm not going to open my mouth anymore tonight."

"Good girl," Grandma Stephy says to her before focusing back on me. "I need to know you understand all of this. That you're loved."

I nod apprehensively, picking at my fingernails. "Okay, I get it."

"And your dad loves you, too," she tries to press.

"Okay." This time, I sound way less sure.

"I know he's not the best dad in the world, but I promise he loves you," she insists, looking a tad apprehensive. "He just hasn't always been able to show it."

"And what about Lynn?" I'm looking her dead in the eyes, so I see the fear flicker across her face.

She swallows hard. "Lynn is ..." She rubs her hand across her face, looking stressed.

"She's not my mom," I answer for her in an uneven voice.

She looks utterly remorseful. "I'm so sorry, Isa. I really

am. I don't want you to hurt, but I guess there's no easy way for you to learn about this."

Her words sink in, though it takes a moment or two for them to really, *really* hit me. And fucking hell, they hurt, like a kick to the shin, a slam of the elbow, a gash to your heart.

"Who's my real mom?" I ask quietly, refusing to look at Indigo, even though I can feel her trying to catch my gaze.

Grandma Stephy smashes her lips together as her eyes well up. "I wish I could tell you, but ..." She kneels down in front of me. "I don't know who she is. Only your dad does ... and Lynn. They've kept it a secret from the rest of the family, which was pretty easy for them, since they barely keep in contact with anyone except for the few reunions they attended."

Her arms circle around me, and she hugs me with everything she has in her. "The only reason I know about any of this is because your dad once asked me to raise you. Your mother ... she couldn't take care of you for some reason, and your dad ... well, at first, he asked me if I could take care of you because he didn't want to put you into foster care. Then something changed, and he decided he wanted to keep you. I tried to talk him out of it, especially because of Lynn, but he's too goddamn thickheaded to listen to anything I say." She leans back and takes my hands in hers.

I realize my fingers are shaking. My entire body is shaking.

"My dad never said why he took me in?" I whisper. "Why he changed his mind? Or why my mom needed to give me away?"

She shakes her head sadly. "I'm sorry, honey, but he never talks about it. The only time it's ever been brought up is over the phone the few weeks before they dropped you off with me, and that's because I forced the subject on him. I was tired of the way they treated you and wanted to get some goddamn answers over what the hell happened fourteen years ago between your mother and him."

My mind swirls with confusion. "Wait ... fourteen years?"

Her hold tightens on my hand, like she's afraid I'm going to run. "You lived with your mother for a few years before you went to go live with your dad."

I press my quivering lips together as tears burn my eyes. "Why can't I remember any of this?"

"Honey, you were barely three when all this happened." Her voice is gentle, yet her hold on my hand is firm as tears slide down my cheeks. "I know this is hard to take in, but—"

I yank my hands out of hers and run to the bathroom. "I think I'm going to be sick," I say, then slam the door shut and lock it.

After I throw up the wine I drank earlier, I sink to the tiled floor in front of my bag. I dig out my sketchpad and open it up to one of my favorite comics I drew, starring me and the woman I always wished was my mom. Maybe she wasn't just a wish, though. Maybe she was a faint memory I was trying to hold on to in dark times.

I touch the dark lines I meticulously drew and whisper, "Who are you?"

Silence is my only answer, and it hurts almost as badly as my heart.

Curling up into a ball, I hug the sketchbook to my chest. Indigo wanted me to spend the summer discovering myself, but how the hell am I supposed to do that when I have no idea where I came from?

After bawling my eyes out for what feels like hours, I finally pull myself off the floor and drag my ass out of the bathroom. The lights are still on, and Indigo is passed out in one of the beds, still wearing her dress, snoring away.

My eyes are so swollen I can barely see anything, but I stand with confidence. I have to in order to hide the nerves sloshing around inside me.

"When I get back, I want to find her," I tell Grandma Stephy.

She quickly aims the remote at the television, shuts off the show she was watching, and rubs the sleepiness from her eyes. "Honey, I'm not sure that's a good idea."

"I don't care if it's a good idea or not." I sit down on

the edge of the bed, still holding my sketchbook. "It's what I want—need—to do. All my life, I felt like I was crazy because I never, ever fit in with my family. And now I learn the reason ... and I want to know who she is, if she's like me. Maybe she can understand me." *Maybe she'll love me.*

Grandma Stephy ruffles her hair into place as she sits up in bed and lowers her feet to the floor. "Isa, I know it's been hard living in that house, but I worry what'll happen to you if this doesn't turn out the way you want it to."

"I don't even know how I want it to turn out," I point out. "I mostly just feel ... lost right now."

She scoots toward me. "I hate to be blunt, but I feel like I have to." She blows out a deafening breath. "There was a reason your mother chose to give you to your father. Whether it's because she couldn't take care of you, or ..." She shakes her head. "I just want you to make sure you think about all the scenarios; how this could turn out before you dive into it."

I get where she's coming from. I can think of a ton of reasons off the top of my head of how this could end up going down. From my real mother being just as mean as Cruella de Lynn to her being dead.

God, what if she is dead? What if I never get to know her? What if I continue to drift through life feeling so out of place?

I have to know; have to understand where I came from, what makes me tick, what makes me so strange.

What makes me ... well, me. And even though I know it might hurt more than anything else, I have to know why she gave me up.

"If I do that—if I spend the next few months thinking about how this is going to turn out—and I still want to find her when we get back, will you help me?" I ask.

She's silent for a maddening amount of time, and I end up chanting one of my songs to keep from shouting at her.

Chocolate fudge. Caramel. Cinnamon rolls. I wonder if my mom bakes ...

"If that's what you decide you want to do, then, yes, I'll help you," she finally agrees, not sounding happy about it.

"Thank you, Grandma."

I feel even more nervous for some reason, now knowing if I can possibly find my real mom. What will I say to her when I see her? What will she say?

"Don't thank me yet." Grandma Stephy points to the other bed. "Now, get some sleep. I have a lot of fun things planned for us tomorrow."

I nod then climb into bed, still grasping my sketch-book. I may have told Grandma Stephy I'd really think this through, but I already know what my decision will end up being. Like Indigo said, good or bad, life is about experiences. And this is one experience I'm going through, even if the outcome is brutal.

CHAPTER SIX

PARIS TURNS OUT TO BE FUN. LIKE, A LOT OF, A LOT OF fun. And we spend so much time sightseeing, tasting the food, and going shopping that I don't have too much time to dwell on my family situation. Still, during the late hours of the night, when Indigo is snoring and Grandma Stephy is tossing and turning, I lie awake in bed, going over every single memory I can scrounge up, trying to figure out how I missed it. Missed the truth. It's hard to take in, hard not to cry, and sometimes, I let the tears soak my pillow.

On the bright side, I haven't received any more strange texts, and my phone has been fairly silent for most of the trip. I'm trying to convince myself that it was just a fluke, a mere wrong number, but I have the most unsettling feeling that there's more to it than that. But I try not to stress about it too much and simply focus on having fun.

We've been in London for a few days now, and there are so many sights to see, like Big Ben and Tower Bridge, that we've had hardly any time to rest. Everyone is feeling the exhaustion, but no one wants to slow down.

"I'm so exhausted," Indigo says to Grandma Stephy as we get on the elevator to go up to our room. "I think I'm going to crash early tonight."

When she catches my eye and gives me "the look," I know her feigned exhaustion is just a ruse. She really has a hidden agenda for us tonight. I'm excited to see what she has planned and cross my fingers that maybe it'll wear me out enough I'll pass out as soon as we go to bed.

"That's okay. I was thinking about going out with some of my friends, anyway," Grandma says as the elevator doors glide open. She steps out into the hallway, and we follow. "Could you two girls do me a favor?"

"Of course, Grandma Stephy; we'd be more than happy to." Indigo lays on her charm thickly.

"Make sure the door shuts all the way when you decide to sneak out." Grandma Stephy grins at us as she digs the key card out of her purse. "Last time, you left it open. You were lucky we didn't get robbed."

Indigo gives her a guilty look. "That was all the way back in Paris. If you knew we were sneaking out all this time, why didn't you say anything?"

Grandma Stephy swipes the key card into the slot on our room door. "Because I didn't want to ruin the fun of sneaking out."

"But you freaked out the one time you found out we left the room," Indigo points out as the three of us enter the small, quaint room. "Why do you suddenly not care what we do?"

"I care. I just figured you two need to have some fun." She looks at me, and I know by that *you two*, she really means *me*. Grandma Stephy sits down to take off her shoes. "But now that we've got that all out into the open, I'd prefer if you two told me where you were going and I didn't have to track you down with that little thing on your phone."

"What thing?" Indigo asks as she unzips her suitcase.

"That little tracker thing that lets you know where your phone is," Grandma Stephy gets up and heads into the bathroom to take a shower.

I flop down on the bed and stretch my arms and legs out. "So, does it lessen our fun that she's known this whole time what we've been up to? Because that whole we're-being-so-rebellious-and-it-makes-this-so-much-more-fun speech you gave when we snuck out to go clubbing seems pretty insignificant now."

"Nah, we still had fun, didn't we?" she asks with her head tucked down as she rummages through her bag for the perfect outfit.

"That we did," I agree, sitting up. "So, what're we doing tonight? Or is it another surprise?"

She looks up at me, grinning as she throws a shimmery black dress at my face. "Tonight, we're going to find you a guy."

I set the dress down on the bed and run my fingers along the glittery fabric, smoothing out the wrinkles. "I don't need to find a guy."

"Liar. You so need to find a guy, so you can get over that Kyler dude."

During a drunken conversation, I told Indigo about Kyler. She isn't a huge fan of my crush on him and said I deserve a guy who actually tries to spend time with me. I wanted to argue that we technically have spent time together, but knew my point was probably moot since a few weekends doesn't really count.

Knowing there's no point in arguing with her, I get up and wiggle into the dress then curl my hair. I apply some dark red lipstick, and kohl eyeliner then add a drop of eye glitter, just because I love looking sparkly sometimes. Since I'm a newbie at the hair and makeup thing, I make sure to get Indigo's approval.

"You look fantastic," she says, admiring my handiwork as she douses her hair in hairspray. "Seriously, you've caught on to this whole makeup and hair stuff way faster than I expected you to."

"Thanks." While I appreciate her approval, there are

times when I still feel like the girl with shiny brown and green hair. Wearing the glittery, probably too short dress, isn't me. I feel like I look ridiculous, and everyone around me knows it.

My phone suddenly buzzes from the nightstand. Indigo and I trade a quizzical look because the thing never goes off.

I hurry over and pick it up, worried there might be something wrong at home. And in the back of my mind, a tiny drop of fear rises that maybe the message is from the unknown caller again.

My confusion only deepens when I see the message is from Kai.

Kai: U haven't sent me any pics yet. :(At first, I thought maybe it's because u forgot all about your cute, sexy neighbor next-door, but then I realized how impossible that could be and started worrying that maybe something bad happened to u. That's it, right? Something bad happened to u?

Me: So you're saying u would rather something bad happen to me?

Kai: Ha! I knew that'd get u to respond.

Me: Whatever. I was never ignoring u since this is the first time u sent me a message.

Kai: I didn't want to seem too needy, but then I realized it wasn't about me. It was about your well-being.

I roll my eyes. I can almost picture Kai smiling as he texts me, totally amused with himself.

Kai: So where's my pic?

"You should probably send him the one we took at the top of the Eiffel Tower. You looked amazing in it," Indigo says, reading the message from over my shoulder. "But first, you have to explain to me who Kai is."

"He's Kyler's younger brother who loves to annoy me," I say, sinking down on the bed.

She coils a strand of her hair around her finger. "Annoy you, huh?" She seems wistful about something. "Because, from what I read through the text, he seems like he's flirting with you."

I laugh so hard I almost pee myself.

"Kai isn't flirting with me. Trust me; he's made it his life mission to annoy the crap out of me." I start to send Kai the pic Indigo suggested then stop myself.

I don't fully understand why. Part of me whispers that my hesitancy is that I don't trust him. The other part of me whispers that I'm just not ready to take these moments overseas, this fantasy world I've been living in where I feel like I can be anyone and do anything, and share it with my old life.

Me: Don't have any cool pics yet. Sorry.

I leave it at that and put my phone away.

He doesn't reply. I don't know why I'm surprised or a tiny bit disappointed, but I am. The sucky part is I don't know what I'm more disappointed about: Kai's silence, or the fact I was too afraid to send him a damn photo.

I shake the feeling off, though, and focus on tonight, focus on my next life experience.

As I walk out the door, my phone buzzes. I fish it out of my bag, and then my stomach ravels in knots.

Unknown: London bridge is falling down, falling down, falling down. And Isabella's world is going to crash down, too.

Panic sets in. My heart slams in my chest. Someone knows about my mom. Someone who knows I'm in London. The only people I can think of who would know that is my grandma Stephy, Indigo, my dad, Lynn, and maybe Hannah.

When Indigo notices my worried expression, she asks, "What's wrong? Why do you look like you're about to be sick?"

Instead of answering, I show her the texts I've received from the unknown caller. She reads over the messages then shakes her head.

"I bet it's Hannah," she says. "It sounds just like something she'd do to you. That stupid bitch. God, I've never been able to stand her."

"Me neither." I clutch the phone in my hand. "But how did she even find out? And how would she get an unknown number? I have her programmed in my phone under her name ..."

"I don't know." Indigo shrugs, not seeming too both-
ered. "Maybe your dad said something about it to her. Or
Lynn. My bet is Lynn. That stupid bitch has always had it
out for you." She shakes her head, her jaw set tight. "And
the whole unknown number thing is probably Hannah's
way of messing around with your head and trying to
make you worry. I bet she just borrowed her friend's or
something so you wouldn't know it was her."

"Maybe." I know she's probably right. If Hannah
found out about my mom, she'd definitely do something
like this to me.

If it is her, I really wish I knew her end game: whether
she's just messing with my head or if there's more to
come.

CHAPTER SEVEN

FOUR HOURS LATER, INDIGO AND I GET IN LINE TO RIDE the London Eye, a ginormous Ferris wheel with oval passenger pods that are covered in windows and are supposed to give you a great view of the city.

Indigo and I met Peter just before we got in line, and Peter just happened to bring along his friend, Nyle. Although, I don't think it was by accident. This is a setup. I get that. What I don't get is what I'm supposed to do with this cute British guy who keeps looking at me like I'm adorable when I can barely focus on anything else other than the text message. I've tried to tell myself to forget about it, to not let Hannah get to me, but I've become obsessed with the idea that maybe she's known I'm only her half-sister for years now, and perhaps that's why she's always despised me.

"You want me to get us a drink or something before we get on?" Nyle asks, tearing me from my stressed out thoughts.

I try to smile like Indigo does all the time whenever she's flirting. "Sure. That sounds great."

He smiles before stepping out of the line to head over to the concession stand.

Indigo gives me a knowing look, and I have no idea how to react. Just what exactly does she think is going to happen on this fun-filled Ferris wheel ride of ours?

I shake my head at her then take in the sights around me; the bright lights, the soft music from the street performers, and the energized buzz in the air.

"It's a beautiful night isn't it?" Nyle asks when he returns to the line.

I tear my attention off the starry sky and catch him checking me out.

He smiles sheepishly at me as he hands me a bottle of Coke.

"Yeah, it's really pretty here." I twist the cap off the bottle and glug down a few swallows, giving myself time to figure out what to say to him.

It's not that I'm shy, but I don't feel as comfortable around him as I do with people I know.

We spend the next ten minutes in awkward silence before we make it to the front of the line and get on the Ferris wheel.

While Indigo chats with Peter about New York, Nyle gets a nervous energy boost and starts babbling to me about himself. I try to listen—I really do—but his opening liner is that he's a math major, and I end up zoning in and out of the conversation, wondering what the hell I'm going to do when I get home.

If Hannah is the one sending me the texts, then she's probably going to make my life a living hell. Well, more than she already does.

I do feel like kind of an asshole for ignoring Nyle. I mean, he's trying to get to know me, telling me about his classes, his love for numbers, canoeing, and water polo, and I can barely pay attention. I nod my head every so often and offer him a few smiles, hoping I'm not coming off as a total bitch. He has to be getting exhausted of me and my silence. At least, that's what I figure when he suddenly grows quiet. When I look at him, though, he's leaning in for a kiss.

"You're really beautiful, you know that?" he whispers, his gaze flickering back and forth between my eyes and my lips. "And a really good listener."

So I've been told, I think as his lips inch toward mine.

I hesitate, deciding. Do I just kiss him, even though I have no interest in him?

The idea seems both appealing and appalling. I mean, on one hand, he's super cute, if you like that preppy, slacks-and-sweater sort of look. On the other hand, I've been bored to death the entire last couple of hours.

"Hey, Isa, come chat with me for a sec, would you?" Indigo interrupts the moment, grabbing me by the arm and towing me to the opposite side of the pod, away from listening ears. "What are you doing?" she whispers, glancing back at Peter and Nyle.

"Um, hanging out," I reply, super confused by the astounded look on her face.

"No, I mean with Nyle," she hisses, unzipping her purse. "It looked like you were about to faint when he leaned in to kiss you."

I scrunch up my nose. "You were watching that?"

"Don't pretend like I'm some pervert. I was just keeping an eye on you, like I promised you I would." She pulls out a tube of lipstick and applies a coat to her lips. "Now, do you want to tell me why you looked sickened over the fact that a hot guy wants to kiss you?"

"I'm not sickened by the fact." I flick a glance in Nyle's direction, and he smiles at me. "I don't know if I should kiss him when we have nothing in common."

She drops her lipstick back into her purse. "Oh, Isa." She ruffles my hair, something she does whenever she thinks I'm being naive. "You have so much to learn."

"About what, exactly?" I comb my fingers through my hair, smoothing the strands back into place. "Kissing complete strangers?"

"About kissing in general." She zips up her purse and rubs her lips together. "Look, if you really don't want to kiss Nyle, then don't. But, if you want to kiss him but you're not because you think kissing should be this fairy tale experience of love at first sight, then I recommend you get over it and give kissing a try."

"But we have nothing in common, and honestly, I'm kind of bored."

"Okay, well, maybe kissing him will make things less boring."

"And what if it doesn't?"

She stares out the glass, the light from the city reflecting in her eyes. "If you kiss him and it sucks, then pretend to sneeze and I'll come rescue you."

"You want me to sneeze in his face?" I struggle not to laugh at the mental image.

"It's the best way to get him to stop. But I think you should give the kissing thing a try." She swings around a couple making out near the center of the pod and heads back across toward the guys. "And, hey, maybe this will help you get over the Kyler thing."

As I make my way back to Nyle, I can't help thinking that maybe Indigo's right. Perhaps I should get over Kyler. After all, he's probably back home, in a lip lock with Hannah.

I wince as I realize how big of a possibility that is.

Then another thought occurs to me. What if he knows she's sending me the texts?

I hastily shake my head. No, Kyler would never be a part of something like that.

Still, the idea of them together sends a rush of anger and adrenaline through my veins. Before I even know what I'm doing, I march straight up to Nyle and seal my lips with his.

He tastes like beer, is the first thought that crosses my mind, which only makes me giggle.

Bravo, Isa, on being the weirdest kisser in the world.

Nyle seems to find me amusing, though, and chuckles along with me before deepening the kiss.

While there's no fireworks or explosions, I do discover that kissing is fun and takes my mind off my problems. I might have to try it again sometime.

Or a lot.

We kiss a lot that night, in the pod, on the street in front of Big Ben, and at a bakery shop we stop at to get cupcakes.

At the end of the night, Nyle and I say good-bye. We don't exchange numbers or emails. We just kiss and tell each other we had fun. There are no expectations to try to talk to each other again, and I like that.

"Was I right? Or was I right?" Indigo asks.

It's well after midnight, but I feel wide awake as we

skip through the glitzy hotel lobby and toward the elevators.

"You were right." I push the up button and wait for the doors to open.

Indigo is grinning like a dork as we jump into the elevator, but her mood swiftly shifts.

"You are having fun, though, right? I just want to make sure that you are. I know after what you found out in Paris ..." She sighs, slipping off her purple platform shoes. "I just want to make sure you're having fun, despite what you found out."

"I promise I am." I link arms with her. "You've done good, cuz."

"Why thank you, cuz." She laughs, slumping back against the wall. "So what did you think of your first kiss?"

"It actually wasn't that bad. And Nyle seems like a great kisser."

"Did it help you forget about Kyler?"

"It actually did for a while," I answer truthfully.

"Good. I'm glad." She presses our floor button with her toe, too lazy to lean forward and do it with her fingers. "You should have seen the look on Nyle's face when you kissed him. He was so into it."

I replay the kiss in my head. The girl in the memory looks like me, yet she's almost unrecognizable, doing things I never thought I'd do.

I look at my reflection in the mirror on the wall. My eyes are big, my cheeks flushed, and my lips are swollen. I look wired, hyped up on life and experiences. I wonder if my family, Kyler, or even Kai would recognize me right now. I think about texting Kai a photo of me and finding out, yet I am too worried he'll know exactly who I am, still see me as the nerdy girl-next-door. And I'm too worried he won't, that through this exterior transformation, I've somehow lost my entire identity.

But that can't be true. I still feel the same. For the most part, anyway. Okay, maybe that's a lie. Deep down, I don't feel like the old Isabella at all. Different, confused, lost—that's how I feel all the time these days. Confused about my life. Over my existence.

I just hope when I get home I'll be able to get some answers so I can maybe feel whole again.

CHAPTER EIGHT

Over the next couple of weeks or so, I try to have as much fun as I can. It's not too difficult, mostly thanks to Indigo and her crazy endeavors.

Like the first time we go clubbing in Scotland. We spend half the night chatting with complete strangers before we head into a club. Indigo orders us drinks then fixes her attention coaxing me into dancing with her.

"You want me to what?" I gape at her like she's a raving lunatic.

She laughs as she picks up a shot glass. "I said, let's dance. We look too hot not to dance."

While I agree that we both look hot in our short dresses with our hair all done up, I don't think dancing is necessary, especially when I can't dance.

"Don't look at me like that. You'll be fine." She angles

back her head, throws down the shot, and then sets the glass down on the counter.

"Yeah, clearly you've never seen me dance; otherwise, you wouldn't be suggesting that." I peer around at the people laughing, drinking, and grinding all up on each other.

"That's a lame excuse," she says. "Give me a better one, and I'll let you off the hook."

The dim lighting makes it hard to see anyone's face, and with the atmosphere buzzing and the music throbbing, there isn't a good excuse I can see anywhere.

I look back at her, sulking. "Do I have to?"

"You don't have to do anything," she says, shimmying her hips as she backs toward the dance floor. "But you're missing out on one of life's great experiences." She raises her hands in the air as she reaches the edge of the dance floor, rocking out to a bass-driven song. "Dance like no one's watching!" she shouts over the music then starts head banging like a freakin' punk rock chick.

I wait for someone to laugh at her then quickly realize no one gives a shit about what anyone else is doing. Everyone's too focused on their own thing, like I should be.

With a deep breath, I gag down my shot and amble toward the dance floor and my crazy cousin.

It takes me a few minutes to warm up and let loose, but I get there. There's something invigorating about dancing like there's no tomorrow. With every laugh, sway of my hips, flail of my arms, I feel more like a different person. Riskier. More daring. Someone who lives life, instead of just existing in it.

So I keep dancing.

I dance until my feet hurt.

Until they blister.

Until I'm so damn tired I can't think straight.

By the time Indigo and I make it back to the hotel, I'm dripping with sweat, tired as hell, but I have a huge-ass smile on my face, totally high on life. Until my stupid phone goes off and ruins the moment.

I don't bother checking the message, already having a pretty good idea of what it will say. That my life is going to break apart. That trouble awaits me at home. Shit like that. I've been getting more texts from the unknown caller over the last couple of days, and it's really starting to piss me off.

"I'm too tired. Hold me up," Indigo whines as we lazily wander down the hallway toward our room.

"No way. You hold me up," I say as she rests her head on my shoulder and leans all her weight against me. "You're the one who made me dance."

"Well, you're the one who refused to stop."

Right as we're about to trip over ourselves, my phone vibrates from inside my pocket again. Dammit! That's the third time tonight.

Unable to stand not knowing any longer, I fumble my phone out of my pocket.

I sigh in relief when I see the message is from Kai, but then tense when I notice I have a few unopened texts from the unknown caller, too.

Ignoring those, I open Kai's message.

Kai: I'm still waiting on that photo. And don't say u don't have any good ones again because I'm not buying it. You've been gone for over two months, and there's no way u haven't taken any good photos yet.

Me: What's up with the pressure? It's starting to stress me out.

Kai: *You're* stressed out??? Think about how stressed I've been. I mean, I haven't heard anything from u except for a few messages here and there, and for all I know, this might not even be u. Maybe some British dude stole your phone and is texting me, pretending to be u.

Me: Wow, that's quite the story u came up with.

Kai. Thanks. I'm pretty proud of it myself.

Me: Well, sorry to burst your awesome story bubble, but I'm not a British dude. I'm just plain old Isa.

Kai: Prove it. Send me the most awesome pic you've taken so far. That's the only way I'll believe u.

"I think he just wants to have a picture of you," Indigo

mutters as she reads the messages from over my shoulder.

"Doubtful."

Me: Can't right now. Sorry.

Kai: I'm seriously disappointed. I was holding on to the hope that you'd finally send me one so I could be entertained at this lame-ass party.

Me: First of all, why on earth would a photo of me entertain u? And second, if you're at a party, why r u bored? Isn't that why people go to parties? So they can be unbored?

Kai: Unbored? Hmmm ... I'm not sure what that means.

Me: Hey, don't mock my awesome made up words. I work hard on them.

Kai: I actually remember that about u. U always tried to convince me that things could be unglittery and unzombie-like. I thought it was funny.

Me: That's because I'm a funny girl. Duh. I thought u knew that already.

Kai: I did ... Still do. Now, please, send me something fun to look at so I can be unbored.

Me: Only if u say pretty please.

Indigo giggles. "Holy shit, Isa, you're totally flirting with him."

My cheeks flush. "I am not."

"You so are."

"So am not … I'm just a little tipsy."

"So? You were a little tipsy toward the end of that night we hung out with Nyle and Peter, and I didn't see you flirting with them." She gives me an accusing look.

My cheeks blaze with heat as I put the phone away without sending Kai another message. "Well, I know Kai."

She examines my face intently, and I wonder what the hell she sees.

"You should ask him for a pic so I can see what he looks like."

I shake my head. "No way. Then you'd try to push me to flirt with him even more."

"Why? Is he hot?"

I shrug. "Sure. I mean, a lot of girls at my school think so."

"Do you think so?" she presses.

I sigh. "Yeah, but so what? It's not like he'd ever think the same way about me."

Indigo targets me with a *don't be silly, Isa* look, something she does a lot. "No guy is that obsessed with getting a picture from a girl unless he likes her."

"Kai doesn't like me." I grind my teeth, thinking about how embarrassed he looked when we were spotted walking home together. "Trust me."

"It seems like he does to me. I think you might just be in denial. You don't think there's any way a guy could ever like you."

"I don't think that anymore." I glance down at my red and black dress and my long, hairless legs. "But Kai hasn't seen me like this. He only knows the awkward, hairy-legged beast Isa."

"Just because you shaved your legs and do your hair doesn't make you a different person," she says as we near our room. "You're still the same Isa who came on this trip. You just have a little more confidence now."

"Okay, so that might be true, but Kai still doesn't like me."

When she gives me a doubtful look, I give her a brief recap of mine and Kai's history.

"Maybe he feels bad about blowing you off now. People do change a lot from when they were thirteen," she says after I'm finished. She uses the key card to open the door then pauses before she walks in. "And it does kinda sound like he's been trying to be friends with you over the last year or so."

I start to protest, but my jaw snaps shut as I hear the sound of moaning coming from inside our room. Indigo's eyes pop wide as the mattress squeaks, and we hear Grandma Stephy groan, "Oh, Harry."

"Oh. My. God." Indigo rapidly shuts the door, and then we both sprint off toward the elevators.

Only when the elevators slide shut, does Indigo finally speak again.

"I don't know what's worse"—she punches the main

floor button—"what we just heard, or the fact Grandma Stephy is getting more action on this trip than either of us."

Laughter bursts from my lips and Indigo quickly joins in. It's the silliest moment ever, and I'll cherish it forever. It's because of moments like these that I've made it through this trip without sinking into a pit of despair over what I learned about my mother.

Yeah, I know that soon I'll be back home and I'll have to finally deal with the truth, but I'll always have these memories, even if some of these moments are really awkward. Through the good, bad, and painfully embarrassing, this trip changed me. It made me stronger, more confident, and hopefully that'll help me when I get home.

I'm laughing so hard by the time we arrive on the main floor that my ribs actually hurt.

"So what do we do now?" I ask as we stumble out into the vacant lobby.

Indigo's gaze skims the front desk, which the receptionist has abandoned, then her eyes land on the pool sign just to our right.

"I have an idea," she says, dragging me toward the doors with a wicked glint in her eyes.

"But it's after hours," I protest, digging my heels into the floor.

"So what?" She swipes the key card through the slot

then tugs open the door. "There's no one here to stop us, is there?"

She's right. There's not a single person around. Why would there be when it's four o'clock in the morning?

The door bangs shut behind us as we step into the faintly lit room that smells like chlorine. The pool gently ripples in front of us, begging to be dipped in.

"What about swimsuits?" I tentatively inch up to the edge, slip off my heels, and dip my toe into the lukewarm water.

"Swimsuits are for amateurs." She shimmies out of her dress then kicks it off to the side. "Besides, you can't cross skinny-dipping off your list if you're wearing a swimsuit."

"Skinny-dipping isn't on my list," I say as she cannonballs into the water, wearing nothing but her underwear and bra.

"The water feels so nice," she remarks as she floats on top of the water, her hair spread out like a veil.

She looks so relaxed, and the water is so inviting.

"Oh, what the hell?" I peel off my dress then wade in.

She's right. The water does feel fantastic. And while the moment is relaxing and not as heart-pumping as dancing in a club or kissing guys on Ferris wheels, it's one I'm glad I lived.

An hour later, we climb out of the pool, dry off, and slip into our dresses. We don't go back into the room.

Instead, we head out to the park across the street where we watch the sunrise.

"I can't believe we have to go home in a few weeks," Indigo says as we rest against each other on a bench near a section of trees.

"I know, but at least we got to experience it, right?" I squint as the sun peeks through the morning haze and lights up the sky.

"I've taught you very, very well, young grasshopper. I feel like such a proud mama right now." She pats my head, and then we both giggle.

We settle against each other and simply watch the sky. I feel so at peace right now with myself, yet I'm afraid at the same time that I won't have this feeling ever again.

Suddenly, I find myself digging out my phone and snapping a photo of me with wet hair and slightly smeared makeup, the sunrise as my background. I have a content smile on my face and actually look fairly decent.

This is who I was once, I type then hit send.

I have no idea why I chose those words other than I'm still a little high on such an amazing night.

A minute later, I instantly regret it, but now there's no going back.

I spend the rest of the morning with Indigo, waiting for Kai to reply.

He never does.

Instead, I get another message from the unknown caller.

Unknown: Almost time for you to come home, and then the real fun begins.

WTF does that mean?

I show Indigo the message, and anger storms in her eyes as she lets out a colorful sequence of nicknames for Hannah.

"Don't worry, Isa; I got your back." She drapes an arm around my shoulder. "Hannah can't do anything to you. Grandma Stephy and I won't let her."

I force a smile, grateful for her trying to protect me. But after eighteen years of being tormented by Hannah, I don't really think it's going to be that easy.

CHAPTER NINE

"OH. MY. GOD," INDIGO GROANS AS SHE STUFFS HER FACE with a double cheeseburger. "I missed you, my dear, sweet hamburger, even though you treat me poorly and go straight to my thighs."

I giggle in the backseat of Grandma Stephy's car then pop a fry into my mouth.

"The food wasn't that bad over there," I say.

She narrows her eyes at me with a drizzle of grease dripping down her chin. "Dude, are you fucking crazy? It was terrible. Everything was either burnt or topped with some weird sauce." She sets the burger down on her lap and dunks a fry into a cup of ranch. "Good God, I've missed ranch on my fries. I'm seriously about to have a foodgasm."

"No foodgasms in the car," Grandma Stephy says as she turns the car off the main road.

I set the fry that I was about to eat down as I suddenly lose my appetite. We're getting closer to my house.

We've been back in Sunnyvale for a couple of nights now, but this will be the first time I've been home in three months. And it'll be the first time I've seen my family since I discovered the secret about my mother.

Time to get some answers.

"Are you sure you don't want to stay with me for a little bit longer?" Grandma Stephy asks for the millionth time.

"I wish I could," I say truthfully. "But my senior year starts in a couple of days, and I need to get stuff ready." I just hope Hannah will leave me alone, that the texts will stop, that she'll give up on tormenting me.

I almost laugh at my own naive thoughts. Yeah, I really doubt that's going to happen.

"What stuff?" Indigo stares at me while she chews on a huge mouthful of hamburger. "We already have your wardrobe fully taken care of. You're seriously going to look edgy hot."

I smile. She's been calling my style edgy hot ever since London when I started wearing boots and leather jackets with dresses and knee-high socks.

"I'm not talking about needing to get clothes. I'm

talking about getting supplies and stuff. You know, pencils and notebooks and books. I also need to get started on my blog again. I haven't done anything with it all summer, and I want to get it going again." I tuck a few strands of my long, brown hair with reddish highlights behind my ear. "I actually think I'm going to blog about our trip."

"Good. It was an awesome trip full of tell-all adventures." She grins at me, and I smile back. "Although, not all of them are tell-all." She points a finger at me, warning me to keep my mouth shut about some of the more interesting stuff we did on our little trip, like our skinny-dipping adventure in the pool.

I draw my fingers over my lips, silently telling her I'll keep my trap shut.

"What are you two girls yammering about?" Grandma Stephy asks as she makes a right into my neighborhood.

"Nothing," Indigo and I say at the same time.

Grandma Stephy shakes her head. "Fine. Keep your secrets. Just know that I have mine, too."

"Oh, we know you do," Indigo says then moans through a giggle. "*Oh, Harry.*"

Grandma Stephy's eyes widen. "What the hell are you talking about?"

"You don't know?" Indigo questions with doubt.

Grandma Stephy rolls her eyes. "How on earth would I know what the hell you're giggling about? You two think everything's funny."

"Only things that are funny," Indigo says through choked laughter. "I know this might be past your time, but the customary rule for having roommates is to leave a tie on the door when you're hooking up. That way, someone doesn't accidentally walk in on something they don't want to see."

The two of them start bantering while I sit back in the seat and watch the homes as we pass them.

I've never been a fan of where I live, and after traveling and seeing so many historical places, Gothic buildings, and even an underground tunnel filled with bones, I kind of hate the homes built to show off the upper-class.

The hatred I feel for the houses dissipates the moment we pull up to my two-story home, replaced by the deepest, nerve-striking anger I've ever felt.

It's going to be okay. Everything is going to change. You're stronger now, and you're going to find out about your mother. Maybe you'll even be able to go live with her.

After my grandma parks the car, I get out, go around to the trunk, and start piling my bags on the ground.

"Here, let me help you." Grandma Stephy shoos me out of the way, takes the last of my bags out, and sets them aside in the driveway. "You want me to help you carry them in?"

I shake my head. "I can do it."

"Are you sure?" she asks, stealing a hesitant glance toward my house, probably afraid to leave me.

"I'm positive," I tell her. "Would you stop worrying so much? Everything's going to be fine."

"You're my granddaughter; it's my job to worry about you." She pulls me in for a hug. "If you need anything at all, you call me, you hear?"

"You're still going to help me, right?" I ask. "You promised you would."

"I told you I'd look into it, and I will, but I really think the best thing to do is talk to your father." She pats my back. "Take a few days and let the trip wear off. Then call me, and we'll figure something out."

I nod, hugging her one last time before stepping away. "Thank you. Not just for the trip, but for everything."

"I just want you to be happy, Isa." She rounds the car and opens the driver's side door, calling out, "And remember, I'm only a thirty-minute drive away."

"Aye, aye, Captain," I holler back.

Laughing, she gets inside the car.

I'm about to start up the driveway when the passenger window rolls down, and Indigo sticks her head out.

"You know I'm going to be visiting at least once a week to make sure you don't go back to your baggy clothes, caterpillar eyebrows, and furry beast legs look," she warns. "And if you're not living up to your full potential, you're in deep shit. I'm talking hours and hours of reading beauty magazines."

My face twists in disgust, but I give her a salute. "Yes, boss."

"And don't you ever forget that." She leans out to hug me. "I can also take care of your sister if you need me to. Seriously, I'm an expert in taking bitchy girls down from their pedestals."

I smile to myself, thinking about how mafia her words sound, kind of like the last thing Kai said to me.

Kai.

I scrunch up my nose. He never did text me back after I sent that photo. I'm not sure why, but it really started to bother me. Not in an oh-my-God-it's-the-end-of-the-world sort of way; more in a why-did-he-bug-me-for-a-photo-if-he-was-just-going-to-diss-me.

My gaze drifts to the house next-door then to my own oversized home. It's weird being back so close to Kyler, Hannah, and Kai when I no longer look like Swamp Thing. But changing my looks wasn't about any of them. I just felt an overwhelming need to change into a person who is more confident and didn't base her looks on the negative comments her mother gave her over the years.

After Grandma Stephy and Indigo pull out onto the street, I hike up the driveway, towing two of my four bags with me.

I can do this. I'm Super Confident Girl, who fears no evil, skinny-dips in the hotel pool late at night, dances in over-crowded clubs, and kisses guys on Ferris wheels.

By the time I reach the back door, though, Super Confident Girl has turned into Freak the Fuck Out Girl. I let go of the bags and stare at the door.

"You can do this, Isa. Just walk on in and tell them to go ..." I bite down on my lip as fear pulsates through me.

"Tell them to go, what?" Kai's amused voice sails over my shoulder.

I sigh. Great. Just what I need right now. Intense, jokester guy-next-door who never texted me back.

"I was going to say *go fuck themselves*," I answer, turning around to face him.

He's rocking his typical look: a pair of shorts with no shirt. His blond hair's a hot mess, and an amused grin is playing at his lips. Then the smile vanishes as he presses his lips together.

His gaze skims across the boots, black floral dress, and leather jacket I'm wearing, lingering uncomfortably long on my bare legs. When his eyes land on my face, I feel like that poser again the one who stepped out onto the streets of Paris wearing that red dress. The feeling has faded over the last few months, but it was easier to be confident with who I am when I was in a club full of strangers who didn't know about my let-my-clothes-swallow-me-up-and-fade-me-into-the-background-of-my-sister's-shadow phase.

"You look ..." A somewhat perplexed, somewhat intrigued look crosses his face, and I seriously get a little excited over what's about to come out of his mouth. "Weird."

"Oh, for the love of God!" I turn back to my suitcases.

Seriously. *Seriously?* All that changing and shaving and tweezing, and I get *weird* again?

"Hey, I didn't mean that in a bad way," he says, though I can hear him chuckling. "Seriously, Isa. I'm sorry."

I hear a *thump* then the sound of footsteps heading my way.

I spin back around then stumble back when I realize Kai is way up in my personal space.

"It sounded a lot better in my head," he says to me as I regain my footing. "But hearing it aloud ... yeah, I'm thinking weird might not be a compliment."

"It's fine." I brush him off. "Just for future reference, maybe you should repeat your compliments in your head a few times before saying them out loud."

"Noted." He smiles again, going right back to his goofy, jokester self. "You know, that photo you sent me didn't do you any justice. I mean, I could tell you looked different, just not this different."

I consider asking him why he never texted me back, but I don't want to give him an opportunity to crack a joke about me obsessing over him.

"So, was the trip everything you hoped it would be and more?" he asks lightly.

I get whiplash from his sudden shift to formality, but whatever.

"Yeah, it was pretty great. I seriously wish I could've stayed longer." Forever, maybe.

"Where did you even go? You said overseas, but that could be a ton of places."

"That's because we went to a ton of places." A smile touches my lips as I remember all the places I saw, all the people I met, how great I felt while on that trip. "My favorite was probably Scotland."

He goes all bug-eyed. "Holy shit, you went to *Scotland?* I thought when you said you were going with your grandma that you'd go somewhere cliché, like Paris."

"I did go to Paris, too, with my grandmother *and* my cousin Indigo, along with an entire old folks' home," I say, shooting him a smile when he raises his brows like *what the hell?* "And FYI, Paris is awesome, and so are old people."

"Maybe it was just you that made the trip and Paris cool," he teases with a cocky grin.

I stick my finger into my mouth and pretend to gag. "That line was sooo cheesy."

"So what? Admit it, you missed my cheesiness."

"Never."

"Not at all?" He fakes a pout. "Wow, way to crush my ego."

I want to tell him no but can't bring myself to do so. Deep down, I might have missed it just a bit.

"Your ego needs crushing."

He beams. "I knew you missed me."

I roll my eyes. "Cocky much?"

"I'm cocky all the time." He pauses, studying me in a way that makes me squirm. "You know, I don't think I believe you that Paris was awesome. I think I need proof." He makes grabby hands. "Let me see some pics so I can decide for myself."

"I already sent you one," I remind him. "You didn't seem that thrilled about it."

"I was too thrilled," he says. "You looked so content in that photo. It made me want to be there with you. I even made it my screensaver."

I resist another eye roll. "You so did not."

"I did, too." He traces an X across his heart with his finger. "But I lost my phone and had to get a new one."

"Are you being serious? Because sometimes, I can't tell."

"You think I'd lie to you?" he questions, jutting out his lip.

When I stare at him, unimpressed, he sighs.

"Look, I promise I'm not lying. I was at a party when you sent me the photo. I looked at it and thought how great of a photo it was. Totally screensaver worthy. So that's what I did with it. Then I went back to the party, totally planning on texting you back and telling you how awesome of a photo is was, but then I got drunk and lost my phone." He shrugs. "Sorry. I really did like the photo."

He seems like he's being genuine, but considering our past, trusting Kai is complicated.

I attempt to get a read on him, but he's doing that smoldering stare thing that makes him hard to read.

"Are you being serious right now about wanting to see all of my photos? Or is this like the time you asked to see my sketches then, when I showed them to you, you told me you were just kidding and looked at me like I was a spaz."

"I never said I was kidding, and I don't think you're a spaz," he says, sounding appalled. "I said I was just teasing you."

"There's a difference?" I ask flatly.

He shakes his head, his lips twitching. "Isa, there's a huge-ass difference between joking around with someone and teasing them."

"Yeah, teasing's way, way worse."

"No, it isn't," he insists. "Teasing is a compliment. It means I like you enough to tease you."

"Well, if that's the case, you must like me a freaking ton, because you pretty much use all of your teasing energy on me. With everyone else, it's all"—I flutter my eyelashes—"look into my eyes and swoon."

"First of all"—he aims a finger at me, fighting back a laugh—"I never flutter my eyelashes."

"You might not think you do, but I've totally seen you do it." I feel oddly gratified that I'm finally getting the upper hand in our conversation. Usually, he always gets me so flustered that I give up. This time, he's the one getting all squirrely.

"Name one time," he says, his eyes burning with fierce determination.

"How about at Hannah's seventeenth birthday party?" I cross my arms and smirk as he grows fidgety. "You were trying to get her attention while she was swimming, and you knelt down on the side of the pool, leaned in, and did this"—I bat my eyelashes—"while whispering something to her. God knows what the hell you said. I remember it made her giggle, and you acted like a cocky asshole for the rest of the day."

His lip twitches, but more out of annoyance. "That was a long time ago, and I was really, really bored that day and trying to piss Kyler off. I thought he had a thing for Hannah. But I'm not that guy anymore."

I choose to be completely ignorant over what he said about thinking Kyler had a thing for Hannah and let Indigo's words about Kai replay in my mind. "*Maybe he feels bad about blowing you off. People do change a lot from when they were thirteen."*

"Are you saying you don't flirt with Hannah anymore?" I ask. "Or you don't flutter your eyelashes anymore?"

"Both," he says, sticking out his hands again. "Now, let me see the photos of your trip."

Sighing, I retrieve my phone from my purse and search for the folder labeled *Trip*.

"My cousin actually took most of the photos. She's into photography, but I did take some." I tap the folder to open it then hand him the phone. "They're not great or anything, but there are some decent ones."

After getting situated on the bottom step of the porch, he starts skimming through the photos, then stops on one of me standing with Indigo in front of a wall of skulls that form a heart. "Where's this?"

"That's the catacombs," I answer, sinking down on the steps beside him, "which are all these tunnels that go under Paris."

He nods, browsing through a couple more photos before he stops again. "Who's this guy feeding you a cupcake?"

"That's Nyle. He lives in London, and he's friends with this guy Peter, who my cousin knew from there."

The photo was to be silly, and it still makes me smile when I look at it.

Kai doesn't say anything else as he finishes looking through the photos. Then he hands me back my phone, rests back on his elbows, and stretches out his long legs.

"Okay, so I didn't want to ask because I thought it'd be rude, but I can't stop thinking about it, so I'm going to ask. Otherwise, I'm going to either lose my mind, or my head's going to explode. But before I ask, I just want you to know that I'm not trying to be rude. I'm just curious." He stops talking. Just like that. After that long-ass speech.

"Dude, are you going to ask, or did you just say all that to drive me crazy?" I ask, stuffing my phone into my pocket.

His eyes sparkle mischievously. "I was just trying to show you how I was feeling. Do you feel like you're losing your mind yet from not knowing the question?"

I pinch his side. I don't even know why I do it. Okay, maybe that's a lie. I saw Indigo use the move on a couple of guys she was flirting with.

Holy shit! I'm flirting with Kai.

What the fuck is wrong with me?

"Wow, you're violent." Kai chuckles, rubbing his side where I pinched him.

"Sorry, I'm just impatient." I clasp my hands in front of me. "Would you please, please ask your question before I either lose my mind, or my head explodes?"

"Fine, I'll ask you." He mockingly rolls his eyes. "Geez, Isa, there's no need to get overdramatic." He flashes me a playful grin when I glare at him, pretending to be more annoyed than I am. "So, what's up with the new look?"

"That's your question? Really?" I frown, disappointed. "I have to say, after all that build up, I thought you'd ask me something way more intense and awkward."

His brow cocks. "Like what? If you're a virgin or something?"

My cheeks flush, and I hate that he can see it. "No, that's not what I was thinking at all."

He grazes his finger across my cheek. "I forgot how cute you are when you blush."

The movement is so quick I barely register it, but my heart accelerates, my pulse pounding against my wrist, my neck—everywhere.

My body is a damn betrayer, and my mind is yelling at me to be pissed off at him. He's talking about the past, back when we used to hang out, and he has no right to talk about those moments he decided to pretend never happened.

"You've never seen me blush before," I lie, my voice a little shaky. I run my fingers through my hair, smoothing it into place. "And I just decided to change my look. It's not a big deal."

"There has to be a reason behind it, especially since I know you hate dresses and makeup and all that girlie shit."

"I've never hated girlie shit. I was just confused …

back then." *Back when you stabbed me in the heart.* "And I'm not that girlie." I lift my feet and tap my boots together. "See? Totally not girlie shoes."

He bites back a smile. "Still, you're way different, and usually there's a reason someone does a complete flip of the switch."

I squirm uncomfortably, thinking about another reason that might have caused my sudden transformation.

Not wanting to sink into my worries in front of him, I turn the focus on him.

I arch my brows. "You mean, like you?"

He grimaces. "Yeah, I guess so."

I consider his question, but the idea of telling him what I discovered about myself and my family while I was on the trip terrifies me.

"I'll show you mine if you show me yours."

His lips quirk up, and his eyes darken. "What exactly are you talking about, Isa? Because when you say shit like that to me, my mind automatically goes right to the gutter." His gaze sweeps up and down my body, causing me to shiver. "But I'm more than happy to show you mine."

I roll my eyes and shove him, laughing. "Don't be gross."

"Hey, you're the one who said it," he says with a grin.

"I meant I'll tell you why I changed if you tell me why you changed."

He considers what I said, but not for very long.

"All right, keep your secrets, then."

"Okay, I will." I'm only a tiny bit sad he won't tell me. I'm curious why he decided to go from jock to this laid-back, I-don't-give-a-shit-about-anything version of Kai. Mainly, I'm glad, not wanting to tell him my secret.

He juts out his lip, pouting again. "You're really not going to tell me?"

"You know that doesn't work on me, right?" I push to my feet, brushing the dirt off the back of my legs. "I gave you a chance to know, but you didn't want to take it."

He rises to his feet and stretches out his arms.

I try not to stare as his shorts ride lower, though I do stare a little.

Unlike Kyler, Kai isn't muscly. Toned, yes. Lean, absolutely.

"Well, maybe I'll change my mind," Kai says, crossing his arms over his chest and stealing my view from me. "Maybe I'll decide to tell you all my secrets, and then you'll have to tell me yours."

"When that happens, then that happens." I give a nonchalant shrug.

"Okay, well ..." He struggles for words, seeming a little unsure of my blasé attitude.

I smile, like, a full-on evil villain, I-just-kicked-your-ass smile. He's so used to getting his way, and I can tell it's driving him crazy that I'm not caving in to his charming smiles and adorable pouts.

"Smile all you want. Just know that I have tricks up my sleeve. I'll get you to tell me when you least expect it."

I raise my hands in front of me and dramatically gasp. "Oh, no. Whatever should I do? Kai Meyers has tricks up his sleeve, and he's going to use them on me." I lower my hands as he glares at me. "You forget, I know the side of you that had magic tricks up his sleeve and dreamed of being a magician."

"You promised you'd never say anything about that," he warns, aiming a finger at me. "And that was, like, when I was twelve. I outgrew that fucking weird phase."

"For your information, I liked that phase," I say, reaching for my suitcases. "You may think it's weird because it's different, but different is so much better than normal." When he gives me a confused yet intrigued look, I ask, "Why are you looking at me like that?"

He shrugs, scuffing his boots against the concrete. "It's nothing."

"It's something." I tug on the bags and start dragging them up the stairs. "You're looking at me like I'm ... I don't know, funny or something. And I wasn't trying to be funny."

"It's not that." He snatches a bag from my hand. "I was just thinking how you still sound like ... you."

"I am still me. Just in different clothes. So stop being weird." I move to grab my bag back, but he dodges out of my reach and somehow manages to steal the other one from me.

"Isa, for God's sake, let me try to be a gentleman," he says, heading for the back door with my bags.

"I didn't know you knew what that word meant." I chase after him, smirking

"I learned it ten seconds ago when I took your bags," he quips, flashing me a haughty smile from over his shoulder as he opens the door. "Don't think this is all out of the kindness of my heart, though. I'm mostly doing it so you'll give me my present." He pauses, waiting for me to confirm I got him a present like he asked.

I want to tell him no, just so I don't have to witness that cocky smile I know he's going to give me, followed by an *"Ah-ha! I knew you liked me."* But I did get him something while on my trip.

When I remain silent, his face lights up. "I knew you'd get me one." His grin expands. "Just like I knew you liked me."

"It's not that great of a present," I try to sidetrack his attention off the meaning of my present. "So don't get too excited," I warn then sigh when he continues to bounce with excitement. "Fine. Take my bags upstairs, and I'll give it to you."

"Wow, that's pretty forward of you." He bites on his bottom lip, trying really hard not to laugh at me.

My damn traitor skin heats up again. "Stop being such a perv."

He giggles. Actually freakin' giggles. And it just might be the adorablest thing ever. I'm not about to tell him that, though.

"You're setting yourself up with these," he says. "Jesus, Isa, what the heck happened to you while you were on that trip? You leave all innocent and come back with a dirty mouth."

I pinch him in the side again, and he ends up dropping one of the bags and it lands on my toe.

"Shit, I'm sorry." He sets the other bag down and reaches to touch me then pulls back. "Are you okay?"

I glance down at my boot. "I'm fine. Totally didn't feel a thing with the boots."

"Are you sure?"

I bob my head up and down, and he smiles tensely, fidgeting as he steps back from me.

Why is he acting like a squirrely weirdo?

"Come on." He picks up the bags again, going right back to the chillaxed version of Kai. "I want to see what you got me."

Nobody's home. That's the first thing I notice when I walk in. I'm not surprised my family isn't here to welcome me home, but it still hurts and makes me want to find my real mom even more. Then again, would it really be better if Lynn, my dad, and Hannah were here, especially with everything going on?

You're going to have to face them sooner or later, Isa, no matter how much you don't want to.

Kai finds his way to my room, with me tailing his heels. I'm surprised he remembers where everything is, since he hasn't been here for five years. But he navigates through the hallways easily and makes it to my room.

The moment he steps inside, though, he frowns. "What happened to all your posters and drawings?"

Confused, I scramble inside to see what he's talking about. The moment I catch sight of the bare and freshly painted white walls, my jaw collides with the floor.

"I don't …" I yank my fingers through my hair as I turn in a circle. "Someone took all my stuff down."

"You didn't take them down?" Kai asks, dropping the bags onto my bed.

I shake my head as tears burn my eyes. "They were here when I left. I don't know what happened."

But really, I do. Either my mom took them down, or it was Hannah's form of revenge. Is this the fun she was referring to in the text? Either way, I'm betting all my posters and drawings are gone forever.

What if they're gone? What if I never see some of that stuff again? As depressing as it is, that stuff was a huge part of my life, especially my drawings.

Reality knocks the wind out of me, and a few tears manage to escape.

"Hey, it's going to be okay," Kai says when he notices the waterworks.

I feel stupid, like a loser again, who cries over ridiculous drawings and posters, because they mean more to her than they should.

"I'm sorry." I wipe away the tears with the back of my hand. "This is so stupid. I shouldn't be crying over drawings, especially in front of you."

"Hey, I cry, too," Kai assures me, pressing his hand to his heart. "And I've cried over drawings and posters before."

"In front of people?" I question, and he hesitates. "See? That's the difference between you and me. You're not crazy enough to cry in front of other people who could eventually use it against you."

"I'm not going to use this against you," he promises. "Seriously, Isa, I'm not that big of an asshole."

"Sometimes, you kind of are, though ... to me, anyway. With everyone else, you're usually so chill. With me ... it's like you get your kicks and giggles out of making me uncomfortable."

He rubs his hand across his jawline, considering something. "Okay, I'll admit I tease you a lot, but only because I'm comfortable around you." When I stare at him in disbelief, he adds, "Well, more comfortable around you than most people." He sighs when I still keep looking at him with skepticism. "Look, when I'm around other people, I'm different. I know this. But everyone expects me to be this intense, serious guy all the time, like Kyler is."

"I hate to break it to ya, but Kyler's not that intense and serious all the time," I say, remembering how much he laughed when we spent those few weeks shooting hoops and hanging out.

Kyler rolls his eyes. "Oh, please. The guy never, ever cracks a joke. Seriously, he's like the most serious person I've ever met. And honestly, he's kind of fucking boring. And you should hear him talk about sports. Talk about a snorefest." He bobs his head back and lets out a snore, emphasizing his point.

I try not to laugh because he's making fun of Kyler and it shouldn't be funny, yet a strangled laugh flees from my mouth.

Kai grins at the sound. "See? Deep down, you agree with me. You just don't want to admit it."

"I don't agree with you," I insist. "Kyler's not boring. He's just quiet and shy."

He makes a choking, gurgling sound then gapes at me. "Kyler's not shy at all, Isa. He's the most arrogant, self-assured asshole I've ever met."

"He might be that way to you," I say, "but to me, he seems quiet and nice."

"Wrong again. He's not nice. Not when you know him like I do." His features harden as he shakes his head in irritation. "My life would be so much easier if he went farther away for college, but no, he has to go here so he can remind me daily who the better Meyers is."

Hmm ... Perhaps Kai's one-eighty transformation has something to do with his brother.

While Kyler hasn't been my best friend or anything, he's always been nice to me, said hi to me in the hallways, and always stood up for me when I was being picked on. Kai, on the other hand, spends most of his time teasing me, and he's never offered me an apology for telling his friend I was a stalker.

"Okay, I get you're not a fan of your brother." I tread with caution, not wanting to hurt his feelings. At the same time, I feel bitter over how Kai treated me in seventh grade. "But Kyler's been nice to me."

"I've been nicer to you more than he has." He shifts his weight, seeming uneasy about something. Perhaps how he treated me in the past? I'll never know, since he won't say anything about it out loud. "Maybe not all the time, but definitely more than he has."

"You've also been mean to me when he never has." My hands shake as I remember the day he ripped out my heart and stomped on it.

"I told you; most of the time, I'm just teasing you." His voice is a drop unsteady as he tiptoes around the big, ugly elephant in the room. "And I only do that because I'm comfortable around you, and you don't expect anything from me." He shrugs, offering me a small, oddly sheepish smile. "You treat me like a normal guy. You never use me to get to my brother." Another shrug, like that's that.

So, he definitely has issues with Kyler. Now that I think about it, I'm not that surprised. Kai always has kind of lived in Kyler's shadow when it comes to sports and girls and grades. It's not like he's not good at any of those things. It's just that he's always one step behind Kyler, almost perfect, but not quite.

He's way funnier. Maybe I should tell him that. Be nicer to him than he's been to me. Try to cheer him up like I used to.

"I'm going to stop you right there," he says. "I can already see you trying to put me together, and no one can put me together, Isa. I'm all kinds of fucked up." He swings around me, right as his phone pings from inside his pocket. Pausing beside me, he fishes his phone out and checks the message.

I don't intentionally try to be nosey, but I catch a glimpse of the opened text on the screen. I mentally scratch my head, because all that's on there is a bunch of numbers, letterings, symbols, and backslashes, like a computer code.

What on earth? Since when did Kai get into computer stuff?

After he reads the message, he puts the phone away and backs for the doorway. "And Isa, you still owe me a present for carrying your bags up the stairs. You better make sure to bring it to school with you on Monday, or I'm going to have to start charging interest." He winks at me before turning on his heels and leaving my room.

The silence sets in as I take in the bare walls around me.

"This is so depressing," I mutter. "There's no way I can look at this for the next nine months."

An idea smacks me in the head. One that will more than likely get me in trouble with my parents, but fuck it. I'm already on the permanent Hate List with them. Besides, I didn't work so hard to become a more confident person just to flush it down the toilet the moment I got home.

CHAPTER TEN

THE MURAL'S GOING TO TAKE A WHILE AND REQUIRES WAY more paint supplies than I have. Plus, I'm not the most fantastic painter, though I do know someone who's an amazing artist.

I pick up my phone and call Indigo.

"Hey, I need a favor," I say after Indigo answers my call.

She yawns. "Dude, Isa, I love you to death, but I just laid down to take a nap."

"Sorry. I'll make it quick." I flop down on my unmade bed and stare up at my lame-ass, boring ceiling. "I need you to pick me up Monday after school then come over to my house and paint a mural on my wall."

I chose Monday because Hannah will be at college orientation, according to the calendar downstairs. And more than likely, my mom will go with her, which means I'll have the entire house to myself for a while.

"A mural?" Confusion laces her voice. "What are you talking about?"

Sighing, I quickly explain to her what happened to my room while I was gone. By the time I'm finished, she's cursed about twenty times and called Lynn and Hannah some very creative names.

"Will you help me?" I ask after she stops freaking out.

"Of course I'll help you," she says, still sounding pissed off. "We're so going to do something badass."

"I have a couple of ideas actually."

"Good. Draw them up, and I'll see what I can do."

"Awesome. And thanks."

"No prob," she says then yawns again. "All right, now I have to go to sleep, or I'll be super pissy when you see me on Monday."

Laughing, I say good-bye.

I don't put the phone away. I have one more call to make before I do.

I punch in Grandma Stephy's number.

"You need me to come rescue you?" she asks the moment she picks up.

"Not yet, but I do need a favor." I chew on my thumbnail then force myself to stop, because it's going to ruin my nail polish. "I know you said to wait a few days and sit on it, but I'm ready to talk to my dad. I can't wait anymore. I need to know."

"Honey, I really think we should wait a couple of days. You never know. You might change your mind and decide to wait until at least you go off to college and get out of that house."

"Someone painted my room while I was gone." I force down the lump in my throat. "And took down all of my posters and drawings. Everything that was me in this room is gone. I need to know what happened. It's all I have left."

"Isa, I'm so sorry. Goddammit, your family's a bunch of assholes," she curses, but when she speaks again, she's calm. "You still have me, sweetie. You know that, right? Just because we're not on a trip together doesn't mean we can't spend time together."

"I know, but I really need to do this. Finding my mom … finding out why she gave me up … I need to know."

Seconds tick by before she says anything.

"All right, I'll call up your father and schedule a time for the three of us to have dinner next week at my place," she says. "He's going to know something's up, though. I'm going to have to lie to him, or he won't come over."

"Tell him that you found something of Grandpa's you think he might like," I suggest. "He's always had a soft spot for Grandpa."

"That's actually a good idea. But how am I supposed to get him to bring you over."

"Just say you want to see me. He's not going to argue, not when Lynn will be more than glad to get a break from me."

"I feel so sneaky right now," she muses through a chuckle. "I like it."

"That's because you're crazy," I tell her, smiling for the first time in over a day.

"I know I am." She pauses. "But, Isa, please promise me that no matter what happens with this—no matter where this goes—you'll always come talk to me. I don't ever want you to feel like you're in this alone."

I press my lips together and nod, even though she can't see me. "I promise."

"Good girl," she says. "And remember, I love you."

"I love you, too."

By the time I hang up, I'm crying. I decide to let it all out. It's better than holding it in and letting it smother me.

Ten minutes later, my eyes are swollen, I have the hiccups, and mascara and eyeliner stain my cheeks. I go to the bathroom to wash my face and fix my makeup before going back to my room and forcing myself to think about something other than my mom.

That becomes increasingly complicated when I hear the front door open. The sound of voices fills the house, and I cringe, deeply considering the idea of staying in my room for all of eternity. Eventually, I'll have to face them, though, so I might as well rip the Band-Aid off now. Besides, maybe I can get to the bottom of where the hell my drawings ended up and if Hannah has anything else planned for me.

Mustering up every ounce of courage I gained on the trip, I square my shoulders and march downstairs. When I enter the living room and see my dad, Lynn, and Hannah all chilling on the sofa, surrounded by tons of shopping bags, chatting about orientation, my confidence goes *see ya later.*

I start to turn around to leave when I hear Hannah say, "What the hell happened to you?"

Summoning a deep breath, I turn around and face them. "Hey."

"Um …" Hannah stares at me with her jaw hanging to her knees, totally speechless.

I fight the urge to cross my arms and try to cover myself up. "So, yeah, I'm back."

"We can see that." Lynn stares at me with an unwelcoming expression, and even though it doesn't seem possible, I swear her eyes carry more hatred for me than they ever have.

I hold her death glare, though, even if my insides are jiggling around like a bouncy house. *I know who you really are. I know where that look of hate comes from. Trust me; I get it. Dad cheated on you, and you hate me, but you know what? You have no right to treat me the way you do, and one day, I'm going to let you know that.*

The longer I look at her, the more she grinds her teeth, until she finally removes her eyes from me and focuses on digging around in the shopping bags.

A sudden, random thought occurs to me then. What if Lynn sent me those texts? She hates me enough, and she's always known I'm not her daughter.

I cast a glance in Hannah's direction. Or was it her? She hates me just as much and has spent years going out of her way to make me miserable.

Dammit! This is driving me mad! How do I get to the bottom of this?

"You look"—my dad scratches his head as he stares at me—"nice."

"Henry," Lynn warns, blasting him with a scowl that could kill. "I thought you said you had stuff to do for work."

"I do." His eyes linger on me a beat or two longer before he stands up and says to Lynn, "I'll be in the office if anyone needs anything." He crosses the room, patting me on the shoulder as he passes. "It's nice to have you back," he whispers before hurrying down the hallway to his office.

Lynn must have heard him because her attention zeroes in on me. "So, *Isabella*," she says my name in the craziest way, like it's an insult. "I see you had a pretty fun trip and got yourself a little makeover."

"You could say that," I reply dryly, sensing a punch line coming.

Her face pinches as she purposefully takes in my outfit. "You should've taken my advice. Dresses don't suit you, hon."

Hannah snickers as she takes out a pair of high heels from a box. "Don't be an idiot, Mom. Nothing suits her."

"Be nice, Hannah," Lynn says, smiling. "She can hear us."

I roll my tongue inside my mouth. I won't cry. I won't.

"What happened to my room?"

Lynn exchanges a fleeting glance with Hannah then looks back at me. "We decided to get it ready for when you move out next year. We're going to turn it into a guestroom."

My fingers curl inward and pierce into my palms. "Okay. But where did you put all of my drawings and posters."

"I threw them away." She pulls out a silver dress from one of the bags. "They weren't in the best condition, anyway. Most of the corners of the posters were torn, and those drawings ..." She lays the dress down. "...well, I've been telling you for years how much I don't like those drawings, and I decided it was time for them to go."

She looks at me with her hands in her lap, her back straight, trying to appear so proper, the innocent victim.

She's not fooling me. I can see the evil villain hidden inside her, the one who hates me and has been trying to ruin my life for the last fourteen years. Maybe that's why I'm really here. Maybe she wanted to punish my dad for cheating on her by torturing me.

"Awesome. I've been meaning to redecorate, anyway." I plaster on a smile that only grows when both their jaws drop.

I should feel more satisfied than I do. I mean, I finally struck them speechless. In the end, though, I have to return to my room where all I have left are the suitcases of stuff I brought back with me from my trip. Sure, it could be worse.

I could have nothing.

But I miss my drawings. I put a lot of time and effort into them. They were part of me and got me through some rough and brutal days.

In a way, the people who starred in the comics were kind of like my friends. Plus, there was the woman, my sidekick, the one I dreamed was my mother. Those sketches are gone, too. And even though I was never positive it was my mom in the drawings, I still feel like I lost a part of her.

CHAPTER ELEVEN

I LEARN THREE THINGS OVER THE NEXT COUPLE OF DAYS:

1. Lynn and Hannah hate my new look. They have made it their mission to destroy any confidence I've gained.

2. The new look seems to have put some kind of confusion spell on my dad. He keeps staring at me like he's trying to figure something out but can't quite get there.

3. The person sending me the texts has gone MIA. I have a feeling that the storm isn't over yet, though. In fact, I have an unsettling feeling things are just getting started, that this is just the lightning before the storm.

To attempt to calm my nerves, I tried to sneak a peek at Hannah's and Lynn's phones, just in case they were just blocking their numbers or got new phone numbers altogether. Lynn's phone was clean of anything weird, but Hannah's phone has a password on it, so I couldn't get access to her texts.

On a positive note, Hannah and Kyler broke up, something I learn when I hear the two of them arguing in the driveway while I'm out drawing on my balcony. From the sound of things, they were never really together to begin with.

"I told you I didn't want a serious girlfriend and that I needed to focus on football," Kyler says to her. "I told you that on our second date."

"And I told you I didn't give a shit," she growls. "You should have thought about that when you kissed me."

"I never meant for that kiss to happen. I told you ... I was a little drunk."

It's too dark outside for me to see them, yet I can hear how uncomfortable Kyler is through his edgy tone.

"I'm really sorry, Hannah, but we're not getting together." He tries to sound firm. "You have to let this go."

When he walks away, I hear Hannah mutter, "Like hell I'm going to let this go. No one rejects me."

I shake my head. Aw, the downfall of being spoiled. She's so used to getting her way she doesn't know how to handle it when she doesn't.

The next couple of hours, I stay outside on my balcony, getting lost in a drawing. I'm not even sure how much time goes by, but eventually my hand starts to cramp up.

"Having fun up there?" Kai's voice floats up from somewhere down below.

Startled, I drop the pencil and lean forward to peer over the railing. "Where are you?"

He giggles like a girl, and I think he might be drunk. "I'm invisible."

I rest my arms on the railing, squinting through the dark until I make out his silhouette in the driveway just below my balcony. "You know, you once told me you wanted to have the superpower of invisibility. Do you remember that?"

"I do remember that," he fully admits. "I'm still working on getting that superpower, though."

"You'll never be invisible," I tell him. "You're just not that kind of guy."

"Hey, maybe I can be … I mean, look at you. You turned un-invisible."

I'm glad he can't see me as my skin warms. "I'm not un-invisible. Nice word choice, by the way."

"Thank you. And that's what you are—un-invisible." As he shuffles backward, the moonlight hits his face, and I can see the swaying in his movements.

"You're drunk, aren't ya?" I tease.

He holds up his fingers an inch apart. "Just a tiny, tiny bit."

"Were you at a party?"

"I was … but not one of those lame-ass parties Kyler always goes to. This party was my kind of party. Not his."

"Okay," I say, again sensing tension between Kyler and him.

"Maybe next time you can come," he says softly. "I mean, I know I'm not my brother or anything, but I can be fun." He drifts off. "Maybe too much fun sometimes …" He dazedly shakes his head. "In fact, I think my fun might have gotten me into some trouble."

"What kind of trouble?" I ask worriedly.

Instead of answering me, he shakes the confusion away and staggers toward the fence that divides our yards.

"See you at school tomorrow, Isa." He clumsily hops over the fence and trips up the steps to his house.

"Yeah, see ya." I gather my things and head inside, trying not to stress over the fact that school starts tomorrow, and I have to go through with my plan to actually try to make friends.

As I lie down in bed to go to sleep, I'm nothing but a bundle of nerves.

I'VE ALWAYS WALKED to school, even after I turned sixteen. While Hannah got a brand new car and a pool party for her sweet sixteen, I got her old bike and a cupcake. And while I was glad just to get something, the old bike does me absolutely no good today as I walk to school in black velvet platforms, not made for pedals. Seriously, what was I thinking?

Yeah, the shoes looked cute when I bought them, and they are, as Indigo put it, "Fucking ama-zing," paired with my knee-high socks, denim shorts, and grey crop tee. But, by the time I reach school, the killer shoes are filled with my blood.

I'm trying not to limp as I cross the crowded parking lot toward the entrance. My attention is on my schedule that came in the mail when I was gone, my thumb is hitched through the handle of my bag, and the wind is threatening to ruin my hair. I'm rocking a side braid with these cool hair rings in it, and I manage to make it safely inside school without a hair moving out of place.

I should probably look up as I start down the hallway, but I want a couple more moments to collect myself before I have to stroll past people who have either never noticed me or noticed me too much, thanks to Hannah. Even though she's now at college, some of her younger friends are still hanging around somewhere. They might be ready to make fun of me, and God knows what they're going to say about that stupid rumor Hannah spread at the beginning of the summer about me being in a mental institution.

"Great, I have math first period," I gripe to myself as I weave my way down the crowded hallway toward my locker with my eyes glued to the schedule. "I hate ma—"

A shiver shoots up my spine as someone grabs me by the waist. Their palms graze the sliver of space between my shirt and shorts, and I just about lose my shit, because I know there's no way it could be one of my kinda, sorta friends touching me like that.

"What the hell?!" I squeal, reeling around and jumping back.

Kai is standing there, wearing a pair of dark jeans, and a shirt for once—we are in school, after all. His hair is a mad mess, but in a bedhead sort of way, and he's biting his bottom lip, struggling not to laugh at me.

"What are you doing?" I hiss, shoving his shoulder.

"Clearly making a scene," he replies, his gaze skimming the hallway.

I glance behind me and cringe. Almost half the people standing near us are gawking, probably because I squealed like a rabid beast. Great. So much for making a good first-day impression and not drawing attention to myself.

Facing Kai, I lightly shove him. "Dude, you can't just grab people like that. You scared the shit out of me."

"When I grab most girls like that, they like it." He smirks.

"Well, I'm not most girls ... and I'm not used to people

touching me." I fidget with a bracelet on my wrist, feeling all sorts of jittery standing here with half the damn school gawking at me. "You feeling better?"

His brows dip. "What do you mean?"

"I mean, better than you did last night. You were a little out of it."

His eyes widen. "I talked to you last night?"

I nod, loving how shocked I made him. "You did. You actually yelled up at my balcony just to get my attention. It was very *Romeo and Juliet*." I shoot him a grin so he'll know I'm kidding.

He crosses his arms and shifts his weights. "Did I say anything ... I don't know ... weird?"

When I shrug, he narrows his eyes at me.

"Nothing too weird," I admit. "Well, other than you declared your undying love for me. Oh, yeah, and for zombies." I smile when he grows even more uneasy. "Relax, you didn't say anything weird. Although, you did invite me to come to the next party with you." And that you might've got into too much trouble, but I'm not sure if I should bring that up or not since he didn't seem like he wanted to talk about it when he said it.

"I did, huh?" He rubs his scruffy jawline, musing over something. "Interesting."

Silence stretches between us, and my thoughts wander back to the people watching us.

I wanted today to go great, but I already have blisters

on my heels, and I screamed in front of half my class. Maybe Hannah was right with what she said to me this morning.

"Once a freak. Always a freak," she sneered when she saw me all dressed up.

I shake my head. No, she's not right. I won't let her be.

I straighten my shoulders and prepare myself. Time to do this. Face the music. Walk in head-on. I just cross my fingers and toes that the majority of the people here have forgotten the rumor Hannah spread. Or that Hannah didn't start a new rumor about me being motherless.

"I have to figure out where all my classes are." I wave bye to Kai. "See ya later. Maybe."

"You've been going here for three years, Isa; you know where all the classrooms are." He snags ahold of my arm and hauls me toward the stairway that leads to the second floor.

I shuffle after him, noting that people are still staring at us. Why, I'm not sure. My best guess is either because of Hannah's rumor or because Kai has his hand on my arm. Sure, he's talked to me in school before, to tease me mainly, but he's definitely never dragged me up the stairway.

He doesn't let me go until we reach a locker toward the end of the hallway on the second floor. By the time his fingers leave my arm, my skin is tingling in the nicest way ever.

"What's with all the touching?" I ask him as I shift the handle of my bag higher onto my shoulder.

He shrugs as he twists the combination of his locker. "You're the one who let me do it."

"I didn't really have a choice."

"You always have a choice."

"Yeah, you're right." I anxiously glance around the hallway, noticing people are still eyeballing us. "But you've never done that in the past. I mean, held my arm in public. Or talked to me." I want to say so much more. I want to point out that back in the day, he wouldn't be caught dead with me. But this doesn't feel like the time or place to bring it up.

He opens his locker, and I spy a bunch of flash drives piled on the top shelf. I'm about to ask him why he has so many when he notices me staring and closes his locker.

"Actually, I have before," he carries on the conversation without missing a beat, which throws me off.

Just what is he up to?

"Or, at least I tried to," he adds. "But usually when I tried to drag you down the hallway to … what did you call it the other day?" He tilts his head to the side as he smirks. "Oh, yeah, 'to get my kicks and giggles,' you pulled away and ran away from me like I was on fire."

I cross my arms, feeling self-conscious. "That's because I knew you were making fun of me."

"No, that was all in your head." He taps his finger

against my temple. "It's all psychological, but now that you're"—he glances up and down at me, lingering extra long on the sliver of skin peeking out of my shirt—"yeah, now you're okay with it, because you're more okay with yourself."

"Is that why you brought me up here? Just to see if I'd come with you?" I ask curiously.

He smiles at me, and I playfully swat his arm.

He places a hand on his arm where I swatted him, laughing. "What's with all the abuse?"

"Sorry, but you're purposely trying to make me mad." I tuck my hands into the back pocket of my shorts. "Now, if you're done playing with my mind, I'm going to go track down my locker."

As I turn to leave, he catches the bottom of my shirt and tows me back toward him.

"I didn't just bring you up here to play with your mind," he says. "You owe me a gift."

"The gift. Yeah, I forgot about that." I slide my backpack off, unzip it, and dig out the small box his gift is in, taking my time just so I'll drive him crazy. When he reaches for the box in my hand, I tuck it behind my back. "Ask nicely."

His eyes narrow to slits, but it's a playful move. "Fine, Isa, can I pretty please"—he juts out his bottom lip —"with cherries and sprinkles and caramel on top, have my present?"

"I'll give it to you, but only because of all the dessert references." I hand over the box.

"You know, you've been promising you're going to give it to me a lot lately." His lips quirk as he opens the box and takes out the leather bracelet engraved with his name on it.

I ignore his dirty remark, though my cheeks warm.

"I got it while I was in Paris. I know it's not anything super awesome, but there was this guy on the street making them, and it made me think of you." I flick his wrist, where he already has an array of bracelets. "I wasn't even positive you'd still be wearing them by the time I got back, since you never used to up until"—I shrug—"well, you changed. I wasn't sure if this bad boy thing of yours was going to be a phase."

He looks up at me, his expression dead serious. "Is this hot girl thing of yours a phase?"

"It's not a hot girl phase," I promise, although my tone's a little shaky. "And no, it's not a phase. But I do need to figure out some stuff."

"What kind of stuff?"

"I don't know. Just stuff."

He stares at me just long enough to make me uneasy then drops the gaze back to the bracelet as he ties it to his wrist. "I like it."

"You don't have to like it." Yet I kind of want him to. "Although, it was way better than the painting my cousin tried to talk me into getting you. You don't seem like a painting kind of guy."

He flicks the bracelet on his wrist. "This is way, way better than a painting." He smiles at me, a genuine smile. "You know what this means, right? You liiiike me."

Biting back a smile, I shake my head. "It so does not."

"Does, too."

"Oh, fine. Whatever."

"Ha! I won that round."

"Only because I let you."

He's grinning from ear to ear. "I like this." He points back and forth between the two of us. "We should do this more often."

"Do what more often?"

Before he can respond, Bradon, one of his stoner friends, strolls up to Kai.

"Hey, did you bring that thing we were talking about the other night at that party?" he asks, stuffing his hands into his pockets.

Kai glances at me, and Bradon tracks his gaze. He blinks, either stunned or high—it's hard to tell for sure, because his eyes are really, really bloodshot.

"Hey," he says, blinking again as he checks me out. "I know you, right?"

I shake my head, trying not to squirm from his attentive gaze. "Probably not."

Kai rubs the back of his neck and tensely glances

around the hallway. I know what's coming. Like the time he was caught walking home with me, he's going to make some lame-ass excuse of why he's here with me.

"I'll see you later," I say, deciding to let him off the hook.

Before anyone can say anything else, I turn around and walk back toward the stairway. As I make my way downstairs, I notice that fewer people are looking my way, but some still stare. I ignore the gawking the best I can, but by the time I make it to my locker, I feel sick to my stomach. I have no idea how I'm going through with my plan of making some real friends when I can barely handle people staring.

Give it time. You'll get used to it. You always do.

That's what I try to tell myself through my morning classes and during lunch when I sit at the same corner table by myself, like I did the previous three years. I get desperate enough that I try to spot Kai at one of the tables. He must leave campus for lunch because I don't see him anywhere. I end up eating lunch while texting Indigo so I won't have to deal with the staring plague that seems to have taken over my school.

I'm not positive what's causing the gawking. I haven't heard any gossip that includes my name, so I don't think the rumor is causing people to act crazy. Still, the thought hovers there in the back of my mind. What if they all think I'm insane? Do I care? I don't want to, and the Isa who was overseas wouldn't, but being back at home, where everyone knows the real me, I kind of do.

By the time the final bell rings, I've made a total of zero friends, and strangely, the handful of people I did talk to during my junior year won't even look me in the eye.

Frustrated, I hurry out of school, pushing my way through the mob of people on the sidewalk.

As I reach the parking lot, my phone buzzes from inside my pocket, so I dig it out.

Indigo: Dude, I forgot how lame high school is.

Me: What r u talking about? You're at school? What school?

Indigo: I'm talking about the lameness of your high school and all high schools in general.

Me: R u here?

Indigo: Duh. How could I not come pick u up after all those depressing texts u sent me?

My gaze lifts to the parking lot, and I spot her sitting on the trunk of my grandma's car with her hair pulled up in a bun, smoking a cigarette.

I run to her. I don't even care how crazy I look at the moment. I'm just so damn glad she's here.

She hops off the trunk, and I hug the bejesus out of her.

"So, I'm guessing by the crazy hugging that your first day totally sucked," she says as she hugs me back.

"It was awful," I tell her. "Everyone kept staring, and even my old friends wouldn't talk to me. The only person who said anything to me was Kai, and that's because he wanted his present."

"Aw, Kai." The tone of her voice implies something. "He wouldn't happen to be around, would he?"

I move back and eye her over suspiciously. "Why?"

She shrugs, dropping her cigarette on the ground and stomping it out with the tip of her boot. "I'm just curious. I mean, other than Kyler, he's the only person from Sunnyvale I've heard you mention. And you're in love with Kyler, so it makes sense why you talked about him. But with Kai"—she bobs her head back and forth, wavering—"I want to find out why he's always so stuck in your head."

"He's not stuck in my head. I talk about him because he's, like, one of the few people who's ever talked to me at school, and that was only on rare occasions." I frown as she stubbornly keeps looking at all the people walking by us. "And I have no idea where he is. I haven't seen him since this morning." I head for the passenger side of the car. "Please tell me you're taking me for ice cream because I'm in desperate need of some sugar."

Her back stiffens. "We actually need to go straight to Grandma's."

I grasp the door handle "Why? Is everything okay?"

She won't look me in the eye, which is completely out

of character for her. "Something happened between her and your dad. They got in a fight and …"

"And what?" I press.

She sighs, meeting my gaze. "And she got a name out of him."

"She did. Yes!" I fist pump the air then hop into the car, bubbling with excitement. Holy shit, she has a name. A freaking name!

I'm so excited I can't sit still.

Indigo climbs into the car and turns on the engine. "Isa, I don't want you to get too excited. Grandma may have gotten a name, but your dad wouldn't tell her anything else. And he's super pissed. Like, really, really angry." She backs out of the parking space. "He even broke a vase."

"That doesn't matter."

All that matters is that I'm about to learn my mother's name. I can do a lot with a name. I can even track her down if I want to, without my dad's help, which I plan on doing.

Because, like I promised myself in Paris, I'm going to find her, no matter what it takes.

CHAPTER TWELVE

THIRTY MINUTES LATER, INDIGO IS PARKING THE CAR IN front of Grandma Stephy's apartment. I have so much pent-up energy inside me that I jump out of the car before it comes to a complete stop. I've done the ninja move before, but never in four-inch platforms, so I end up rolling my ankle and eating asphalt as I fall to the ground.

"For the love of God." I clumsily push to my feet and look at the damage.

My knee is bleeding and pebbles are stuck in the open cut. I think a piece of glass might be in there, too. I almost throw up.

I'm cool with seeing blood and gore on television, but it's a whole different story when the blood's gushing out of me.

Determined to make it inside, I force the vomit back and pluck out the glass.

"Oh, my God ..." Oxygen is ripped from my lungs as more blood trickles out of the wound.

"Jesus, Isa, are you okay?" Indigo rushes around the front of the car toward me.

"I'm totally fine." *I can do this. Be tough.*

I take off, limping up the sidewalk toward my grandma's place.

"Isa, would you please slow down?" Indigo's sandals scuff against the ground as she jogs to catch up with me. "You're leaving a trail of blood all over the ground, for God's sake."

I look down and, sure enough, blood is dripping out of the cut, down my leg, and onto the concrete. I gag, but fuse my lips together.

"Holy shit, I think you might need stitches," Indigo remarks as she bends over and squints at the open wound.

"The stitches can wait until I talk to Grandma." I hobble toward the apartment again, refusing to look down at the cut.

Cotton candy. Gummy worms. Licorice. I chant in my head, trying to stay calm.

"You're going to end up with a scar if you don't take care of it," Indigo points out, stopping by the front door to light up.

"I'll take care of it." I open the apartment door and stumble into Grandma Stephy's living room.

She's sitting on the couch, surrounded by tons of used Kleenexes, and her head is in her hands.

When I enter, she quickly looks up, blinking her puffy eyes. "Oh, my God, I'm so sorry." She stands up and winds around the coffee table toward me. "I think I messed up."

"Indigo says you got a name. Please tell me that's true." I hunch over and place my hand on my knee.

Now that the adrenaline rush is fading, the pain is becoming way more knock-me-on-my-ass intense, and the vomit burning at the back of my throat is harder to keep down.

"He accidentally let it slip out when he was yelling at me," she says with a cautious edge to her voice. "I'm not even sure he realized he said it."

Unable to stand any longer, I sink down on the floor and straighten my knee. "What happened, anyway? Why was he even here? I thought we were going to do this together?" I blink a few times as everything around me spins.

"Honey, what did you do to your leg?" She kneels down on the carpet beside me to examine the cut on my knee. "My word, Isa. This looks really, really bad."

"I jumped out of the car and fell." I slump back, resting my head against the door. "Please, Grandma Stephy, just tell me her name." *Breathe in. Breathe out. Breathe through the pain.*

"Her name is Bella," my grandma says right before I pass out.

WHEN MY EYELIDS FLUTTER OPEN, my eyes are instantly assaulted by florescent light; the smell of cleaner attacks my nostrils; and my knee feels like a zombie took a bite out of it.

"Where the hell am I?" I mutter as I sit up.

"Easy, Isa." My grandma Stephy appears by my bedside, looking paler than normal. "We had to take you to the hospital."

I take in the privacy curtain, the thin bed I'm lying in, and Indigo sitting in a chair. "How'd I get …" I cup my head then my mouth sinks. "Oh …" The last few hours rush back to me.

Grandma Stephy pats my hand that's resting on my waist. "You've never been good with blood. You worried me to death when you blacked out."

I look down at my knee, which is now wrapped in a bandage, thank God. "Did I have to get stitches?"

"You did." Grandma Stephy smoothes my hair from my forehead so she can look me in the eyes. "How are you feeling? About *everything*?"

"The leg hurts," I admit. "And the thing with my mom … you said her name is Bella." I smile at that. "I have to be named after her, right?"

"I guess so." Grandma Stephy glances over her shoulder at Indigo. "Honey, would you mind going and getting me a soda from the vending machine?"

Indigo nods and Grandma Stephy waits until she ducks out from the curtain before she sits down on the edge of the bed.

"Isa, your dad knows I told you about your mom. That's why he came over to my house today."

"How did he find out? I didn't say anything to him."

"You didn't have to. He said he knew from the moment you got back from your trip. He said you looked so much like her, and he just jumped to the conclusion that your change came from learning who your mom is."

"I look like her?" I try not to act too giddy since Grandma Stephy seems upset, but I can't help it. I'm totally freakin' excited!

"According to your dad, you do." She gazes off into empty space. "I can't believe how your father acted today. I mean, I always kind of knew he was a spoiled brat. But …" She looks back at me. "Your grandpa used to spoil him all the time because he was his only son. Everything Henry wanted, your grandpa gave him. I knew one day it would backfire. The way he treated me"—she shakes her head—"I just can't believe that man yelling at me today is my son."

"I'm sorry. I feel like this is all my fault."

"It's not your fault. He never should've kept you in the dark like he did. What I don't get is how on earth he thought I told you how your mother looked, and all the other stuff he was saying. He acted like I somehow found out everything about her and told you."

"Maybe he thought you hired a private investigator." I shift my leg into a more comfortable position as the low ache ignites into a fiery pain.

"Maybe." She mulls over something, tousling her short hair with her fingers. "I don't know, though. I'd have to have a starting point for that, which I don't."

"But there has to be a starting point. I mean, if she had me and I lived with her for a while, it'd be documented, like say … with a birth certificate."

"You sound like a mystery novel right now, Isa," she says with a thoughtful smile.

"Well, I do read them a lot," I admit. "But I'm just saying, her name has to be on it, doesn't it?"

She promptly shakes her head. "I know where you're going with this, and the answer is no."

I give her my most innocent look, my lips parting, my eyes widening. "I have no idea what you're talking about."

"Your father is already upset as it is," she continues, ignoring me. "If he caught you snooping around …" She shakes her head in dismay. "I don't even want to go there."

"He's not going to hurt me, if that's what you're thinking."

"I know he won't hurt you, but with how they treat you now, and if Lynn gets involved in this …" She sighs heavily as she checks the screen of her phone. "I really think you should reconsider my offer to come live with me. Your father won't be happy about it. That doesn't mean I can't fight it, though. He's proved way too many times that he doesn't deserve to have you around."

"I don't think he'd care," I say, repositioning my leg.

"I wouldn't be so sure of that," she tells me with a heavy-hearted look. "In fact, he might have mentioned something about me staying away from you while he was mad. And he's probably going to yell at me when he gets here."

My mouth curves down into a frown as my shoulders slump. "He's headed here? Why?"

"Because he's your guardian and you're on his insurance." She covers her hand over mine. "Don't worry; he's just going to be angry with me."

"Well, I'm going to let him know this is all my fault." I grip her hand, trying to tell myself that everything will be okay. "I'm sure once he realizes that, he'll let me see you again." Besides, there's no way Lynn would ever let my dad try to keep me at our house.

"I'm not sure he's going to change his mind about this. Usually, I'd say yes—that his threat was one of his temper tantrums—but this time, he seems pretty dead set on you keeping your distance from me." Determination fills her eyes. "I can make it happen, Isa. Just say you want to live with me, and I'll make sure to get you out of that house."

I take in her kind eyes that have dark circles under them and her pale skin. She looks way more worn out than the Grandma Stephy I know. The fight she had with my dad today must've gotten to her more than she's letting on.

"I'm fine," I assure her as confidently as I can. "Besides, I don't want to have to change schools and be known as the new girl for my senior year."

"You never know; being the new girl might give you a chance at a fresh start, which was what you and Indigo were always yammering about during the trip. Every damn night, that's all I heard while I tried to fall asleep." She tries to appear annoyed, but a trace of a smile forms on her lips.

She's right. Starting a new school could give me a fresh start. And, hey, maybe I'd even make some new friends and no longer have to be Loner Girl. But putting more stress on Grandma Stephy is definitely something I don't want to do.

"Can we talk about me living with you in a couple of weeks? Maybe after my dad's cooled off? He might be more willing to agree to let me go then." I'm almost certain he will. It's not like he wants me there, anyway.

"Maybe." She sounds pretty skeptical, though, which makes me wonder exactly what was said during their argument. Her shoulders slump forward as she sighs. "If that's what you want. But only if you promise to call me the moment things get too bad."

Things have been bad for years now. I don't point that out, though.

"All right, I promise." And just because I know it'll make her smile, I stick out my pinkie. "In fact, I pinkie swear."

She shakes her head, but a smile breaks through. She hitches her pinkie with mine.

The moment we pull away, my dad comes storming in.

He looks at Grandma Stephy as he points toward the exit. "Get. Out. Now."

"Watch your tongue, young man." Grandma Stephy collects her purse from a chair and slings the handle over her shoulder. "You might think it's okay to talk to your mother like that, but it's not. You *will* respect me."

"I'll respect you as much as you respect me," he growls, stepping toward her. "Telling Isa what you did, you had no right."

"I'm not going to get into this with you again," she

replies as calmly as she can. "I'm going home, and I'll call you in a few days when you've calmed down."

"Don't call ever again!" he shouts after her as she walks out of the room. "And you're never to see Isa again."

"Dad, stop," I hiss. "Leave Grandma alone. She didn't do anything wrong."

My dad's attention whips back to me and, by the anger in his eyes, I expect him to yell at me. When he speaks, though, he's unsettlingly composed.

"We're not going to talk about this ever again. No mention of it, okay?"

I shake my head. "No, I'm going to mention it. A lot. And I'm going to bug you until you tell me who my mom is."

He ignores me, his back as stiff as a board. "I'm going to get the doctor."

Before I can get another word out, he leaves the room.

I grit my teeth, more furious than I've ever been.

I make another vow to myself right then and there that the second I get home, I'm going to get my hands on my birth certificate.

I'm going to solve this mystery once and for all.

ABOUT THE AUTHOR

Jessica Sorensen is a *New York Times* and *USA Today* best-selling author who lives in the snowy mountains of Wyoming. When she's not writing, she spends her time reading and hanging out with her family.

ALSO BY JESSICA SORENSEN

The Sunnyvale Mysteries:

Isa & the Guy Next Door

Isa & the Mystery

Isa & the Deal

The Year of Love & Whispered Truth

The Year of Promises & First Kiss

Untitled (coming soon)

The Unexpected Series:

Ensley & the Popular Guy

Untitled (coming soon)

The Honeyton Mysteries:

Hadley & the Guy Next Door

The Deal & a Secret

The Mystery & a Kiss

Untitled (coming soon)

The Alexis Files:

Sweet Little Lies

Truths & a Mystery

Secrets & the Spies

Confessions & a Secret (coming soon)

My Life with the Band

Discovering Benton

Whispered Secrets & a Kiss

Untitled (coming soon)

The Illusion Series:

The Illusion of Annabella

The Mysteries of Star Grove

Suspicion

Untitled (coming soon)

Rules of Willow & Beck:

Rules of Willow & Beck

Untitled (coming soon)

The Confession of Luna:

The Confessions of Luna

Untitled (coming soon)

Secrets Never Die:

Secrets Never Die

Untitled (coming soon)

Lexi Ashford Series:

The Diary of Lexi Ashford

The Diary of Lexi Ashford: The Agreement

Untitled (coming soon)

The Heartbreaker Society:

The Opposite of Ordinary

The Simplicity in Ordinary

Untitled (coming soon)

The Unraveling Mysteries Series:

The Mysterious Guy Next Door

The Mystery of the Symbol

The Forgotten Memory

The Suspicious Note

Untitled (coming soon)

A Pact Between the Forgotten:

The Art of Being Friends

The Rules of Being Friends

The Art of Kissing (coming soon)

Shadow Cove Series:

Spies & Sprinkles

Secrets & Vanilla Bean Frosting (coming soon)

The Coincidence Series:

The Coincidence of Callie and Kayden

The Redemption of Callie and Kayden

The Destiny of Violet and Luke

The Truth of Violet and Luke

The Promise of Violet and Luke

The Evermore of Callie and Kayden

Seth & Greyson

The Coincidence Mysteries:

Callie & the Start of a Mystery

Untitled (coming soon)

The Secret Series:

The Prelude of Ella and Micha

The Secret of Ella and Micha

The Forever of Ella and Micha

The Temptation of Lila and Ethan

The Ever After of Ella and Micha

Lila and Ethan: Forever and Always

Ella and Micha: Infinitely and Always

The Secret Star Grove Mysteries:

Ella & the Interrupted Road Trip

Ella & the Welcome Home

Untitled (coming soon)

Breaking Nova Series:

Breaking Nova

Saving Quinton

Delilah: The Making of Red

Nova and Quinton: No Regrets

Tristan: Finding Hope

Wreck Me

Ruin me

Unbeautiful Series:

Unbeautiful

Untamed

Tangled Realms:

Forever Violet

Untitled (coming soon)

Harlynn's Mystery Investigations:

Sugar Cookies & Zombie Secrets

Untitled (coming soon)

Mystic Willow Bay Vampires

Tempting Raven

Enchanting Raven

Alluring Raven

Untitled (coming soon)

Mystic Willow Bay Mysteries Series:

The Secret Life of a Witch

Broken Magic

Stolen Kisses

One Wild, Crazy, Zombie Night

Magical Whispers & the Undead

Untitled (coming soon)

Enchanted Chaos Series:

Enchanted Chaos

Shimmering Chaos

Iridescent Chaos (coming soon)

Capturing Magic:

The Thief of Wishes

The Thief of Magic

Untitled (coming soon)

My Cursed Superhero Life:

Grim

Untitled (coming soon)

Guardian Academy Series:

Entranced

Entangled

Enchanted

Entice

Charmed

Untitled (coming soon)

Monster Academy for the Magical:

Monster Academy for the Magical

Monster Academy for the Magical: Hidden Magic

Monster Academy for the Magical: The Monster Trial

Untitled (coming soon)

The Shattered Promises Series:

Shattered Promises

Fractured Souls

Unbroken

Broken Visions

Scattered Ashes

The Fallen Star Series:

The Fallen Star

The Underworld

The Vision

The Promise

The Lost Soul

The Evanescence

The Mist of Stars (untitled)

The Darkness Falls Series:

Darkness Falls

Darkness Breaks

Darkness Fades

The Death Collectors Series (NA and YA):

Ember X and Ember

Cinder X and Cinder

Spark X and Spark

Standalones:

The Forgotten Girl